Is this love. . .so soon?

Sitting in his chair, leaning back with his arm still resting on top of his head, Ken watched Molly. He'd seen so many different facets of her personality yesterday, and it had only served to strengthen how he felt about her.

The woman who had grabbed him by the hand and forcefully pulled him out of the petting zoo had burst into tears over the simple but meaningful words of a children's song. The woman who had charmed his company's most important client had talked to a pig. He didn't want to compare her one-sided conversation with the little animal to his own rather one-sided conversation with her at lunch. Then, for a complete turnaround, instead of a diet of nonstop chatter, during their journey through the aquarium they'd shared a very comfortable silence as they walked slowly through the complex.

Since it had been busy, at one point he had held on to her hand so they wouldn't become separated in the crowd. When the crowd thinned, he hadn't let go, and Molly hadn't pulled away. They'd spent much of their visit walking around the exotic fish and aquatic displays hand in hand, and he'd thoroughly enjoyed himself. The aquarium had been interesting, but being with Molly in the dark complex lit only by the backlight from the aquariums made it enchanting.

The only thing that would have made a great day perfect would have been if he could have kissed her when he left.

He was completely and totally in love with Molly. Now if only he could figure out what to do about it.

GAIL SATTLER was born and raised in Winnipeg, Manitoba, and now lives in Vancouver, BC (where you don't have to shovel rain) with her husband, three sons, dog, and countless fish, many of whom have names. Gail became a Christian with her husband after he joined AA. She began writing when the company she worked for closed and she chose to stay home with her children. She writes inspirational romance because she loves happily-ever-afters and believes God has a place in that happy ending. She now works part time as office manager for a web design company. Visit Gail on the Internet at www.getset.com/gs

Books by Gail Sattler

HEARTSONG PRESENTS
HP269—Walking the Dog
HP306—Piano Lessons
HP325—Gone Camping

Don't miss out on any of our super romances. Write to us at the following address for information on our newest releases and club information.

Heartsong Presents Readers' Service
PO Box 719
Uhrichsville, OH 44683

At Arm's Length

Gail Sattler

Heartsong Presents

Dedicated to my son Chris, who is my "lefty."

A note from the author:
I love to hear from my readers! You may correspond with me by writing:

Gail Sattler
Author Relations
PO Box 719
Uhrichsville, OH 44683

ISBN 1-57748-702-8

AT ARM'S LENGTH

All Scripture quotations are taken from the Authorized King James Version of the Bible.

All of the characters and events in this book are fictitious. Any resemblance to actual persons, living or dead, or to actual events is purely coincidental.

Cover illustration by Ron Hall.

PRINTED IN THE U.S.A.

one

"Miss McNeil, could I see you in my office right away, please?" The intercom speaker echoed with a loud click as the company's president hung up.

Molly cringed. As receptionist, she couldn't leave the reception area unattended, but suddenly, Janice appeared to relieve her when she hadn't been the one to ask.

Molly's breath caught in her throat. Rumor had it that big changes would soon be happening, and that usually meant downsizing. Would she be the first to go? With trembling hands, she dug out her notepad and pen and walked to Mr. Quinlan's office. She thought this would probably be a good time to pray, but beyond begging God to allow her to keep her job, her mind went blank.

"Come in. Sit down."

She tried her best to smile, but it fell flat. Molly sat in the chair in front of his large desk, grateful for the chance to take her weight off her wobbly knees. Mentally, she started calculating how long she could survive on her meager savings before she found another job.

Mr. Quinlan folded his hands on the polished metal desktop. Absently, she compared the shiny surface to his bald head. He flipped through a file. Her personnel file. Molly started to feel sick.

"You started in the mailroom, moved to file clerk, spent some time as. . . ," he flipped the page, ". . .junior clerk in payables. You've been the receptionist for a few years, now." He closed the folder and sat back in his chair, resting his hands on his protruding belly.

Her experience at Quinlan Enterprises wouldn't make an impressive resume, but perhaps the business courses she'd

5

completed at night school would impress a future potential employer. She had hoped to be able to work her way up, but it now looked like the only place she was going was out the front door.

"Uh, yes. . . ," she mumbled, forcing the words out.

He checked his wristwatch. "Janice will take over your current projects effective immediately. Have you removed your personal effects from the desk?"

Now she really felt sick. "No. . ."

He leaned forward, clasping his hands and resting them on top of her now closed personnel file. He opened his mouth to speak but was interrupted by a knock on the office door as it opened. A young man in an expensive suit hustled in and shut the door behind him.

"Sorry I'm late. You wouldn't believe the traffic." He glanced her way briefly, then turned to face Mr. Quinlan.

Molly forced herself to breathe. Mr. Quinlan acknowledged him with a nod. The young man, whoever he was, turned to smile a greeting at her, showing the cutest set of dimples and adorable crinkles at the corners of his eyes. His tall frame filled out the tailored suit to perfection, showing off broad shoulders and trim hips, a build that shouldn't have been confined in a suit.

Molly stared at him, transfixed by his eyes. A dark steel blue, the cool color oddly radiated a warmth that instantly led her to trust him. They contrasted perfectly with his black hair, which was meticulously cut and combed back, heightening his soft but still very masculine features.

As he lowered himself into the chair beside her, smiling the entire time, their gazes locked. Now that he was so close, she detected a spicy delicious male fragrance. Molly didn't usually like cologne on men, but this time, if she hadn't been already sitting and if this had taken place a hundred years sooner, she wondered if she might have fallen to the ground in a swoon. She told herself she was being ridiculous.

She hoped she wouldn't be asked to speak, because she

didn't know if she could.

Mr. Quinlan nodded. "Molly McNeil, this is my nephew, Kenneth Quinlan."

The junior Mr. Quinlan shuffled to turn his body toward her as she remained sitting and extended his hand, no doubt expecting her to respond.

She couldn't understand why she was being introduced to the owner's nephew when she was on her way out.

For five years she'd worked at Quinlan Enterprises. Molly knew every nook and cranny, every storage space, and she'd learned the location of almost every file in the building during her stint as filing clerk and office gopher. Later, when she took the receptionist position, she had made it a priority to know all the staff's job descriptions so she could best transfer calls to the correct person the first time and to know enough to ask the right questions to take intelligent messages. It was something she took pride in, and that knowledge should have made her more valuable, not the first person to be fired. It only hurt worse to know she was being replaced by a junior employee.

She responded by giving him the limpest handshake of her life.

"Pleased to meet you, Miss McNeil. Or may I call you Molly? Whichever you prefer, of course."

"M. . .M. . .Molly." She blinked at him, then continued to stare at him like he was from outer space.

As he held onto her hand, Ken studied her. This was one woman who would not go unnoticed. Her flaming red hair would set her apart in any crowd. It was a shade he'd never seen before, a shocking orange-red in a wild array of curls he could only compare to Little Orphan Annie, in an adult sort of way.

In contrast to her vivid hair, her clothing was businesslike and conservative, a nice neutral shade that set the color of her hair even more apart. He didn't know much about women's hair, but as unique as the color was, he doubted it came from a bottle. As with every redhead he'd ever met, she, too, had green eyes and a smattering of freckles across her pert little nose. She was cute and fresh-looking, her expression unguarded and transparent as she stared at him in open astonishment.

"And please call me Ken, after all, we're going to be seeing a lot of each other."

As Ken slowly released her hand, her face paled, making him worry that something was terribly wrong. Since his plane was late, he'd phoned from the airport. Uncle Walter had said it wasn't a problem; he would be introduced to the person who would be showing him around when he finally arrived. However, she didn't seem too enthusiastic.

"We are?" she stammered, then glanced back and forth between himself and Uncle Walter with big round eyes.

Uncle Walter knotted his eyebrows. "Didn't Theresa speak to you this morning, Molly?"

"Uh, no. . ."

"Theresa was supposed to tell you that we've selected you to be Kenneth's assistant until he gets settled."

"Me? His assistant? That's what you called me in here for?" She sat completely still for a few seconds, then burst out into a very strange humorless laugh.

Personally, Ken thought himself a nice guy, and the job of showing him around shouldn't be so unnerving to cause anyone to react so strangely. He struggled not to give away any indications of his bruised ego.

Uncle Walter stood. "Well, Kenneth, I know you said you'd be happy with the back desk in the accounting department, but you know Nancy volunteered to let you use her office."

Ken stood in response. He hated being called Kenneth, although it was a step up from being called Kenny, the hated childhood name he'd only managed to shake when he turned twenty-five. He hoped it didn't take another twenty-five years to be referred to as just plain Ken, because if so, he had another twenty-three years to go.

"I told you, I don't want to be in the way, and I don't want to disrupt the status quo. The back desk will be fine." He turned to Molly. "Before we start, I do have a few things to take care of, and I have a number of boxes in Theresa's car."

His uncle tipped his head slightly, turning again to Molly. "Since you're going to be working closely with Kenneth, you'll have the empty desk beside his. We just have to move the things stored in it, and it will be yours. Perhaps you could find a home for those old files and move your personal effects while Kenneth gets settled."

Ken extended his hand to Molly again. This time, she grasped his hand firmly, making him not want to let go. Her hand was small and soft, and this time, all the color had returned to her face as she returned his handshake. "I'm looking forward to working with you, Molly. See you in about half an hour."

With that, he turned and headed for the parking lot.

～

Molly watched him go until he disappeared through the opening to the lobby. His assistant? She couldn't imagine what she might be able to show him that he wouldn't already know. Ken Quinlan had been running the Winnipeg production plant for the past two years, so he was more than familiar with the company and the way things ran. Even though she couldn't remember ever having seen him before, she didn't think there would be much, if anything, he didn't already know.

And she wondered what he was doing here. Unless she was wrong, it appeared his move was permanent. So far she hadn't seen an announcement that they'd hired a new manger for his old position, but that didn't mean there hadn't been one. She wondered how to find out what was going on, and how it could possibly involve her.

Mr. Quinlan's voice broke her mental ramblings. "I'll speak to Theresa about not informing you of our decision. My apologies."

Molly struggled to contain her blush as Mr. Quinlan shook

her hand. She'd never had such an important person apologize to her before. Come to think of it, hardly anyone had ever apologized to her before, except for her brother, and most of the time that was far from voluntary. "I guess I should work on clearing out that desk, then."

She took her leave and headed for her temporary desk, dreading what she would find. Whenever anyone had old files or archives too difficult or inconvenient to put away, everyone stashed them inside the drawers in the spare desk where no one could see, so she doubted Mr. Quinlan knew what he was asking. It was only when the filing department had time that those old files were eventually returned to their rightful place in the storage areas or in the attic. It would take far longer than half an hour to clear even a portion of what had collected over time.

During her many trips back and forth to the back of the storage room, she overheard whisperings of gossip about her new position. Apparently she was the last to know. She couldn't help but also overhear jealous complaints from a few of the single women.

The thought that someone of his background of money and privilege would be interested in her was preposterous. She was only a lowly office clerk. He was family.

The half hour passed too quickly. She was nowhere near ready when Ken signaled his readiness to start. She left everything scattered in haphazard piles and abandoned the mess to be sorted later. First, Molly formally introduced him to everyone individually, allowing a few minutes to chat at each stop. Before she knew it, it was lunchtime.

Standing at the two disorganized desks in the rear corner of the office, Molly bent to reach for her purse, when a light touch on her arm made her breath catch.

"Molly, may I take you out for lunch? I regret that we didn't have time to talk before being thrown together. I'd welcome the opportunity to get away from the rest of the staff and listen to your ideas, and I'll let you know my goals. I'd prefer we talk in private. Or do you have other plans?"

Actually, she did have other plans, but she wanted to get off on the right foot with the boss's nephew, especially now that he was her immediate supervisor. "I just have a few errands, I can always do them after work."

He smiled, and her heartbeat quickened. Molly tried to smile back without looking like a simpering fool and wondered how long it would take to get used to him.

Rather than drive, since he'd been sitting for hours on the plane, they walked a few doors down to a small Italian restaurant that specialized in quick lunches for their business-oriented clientele. They were soon seated at a small corner table.

Molly folded her hands in front of her and waited for him to speak, preparing herself to listen to him outline her expected duties. Instead, he asked her general questions about procedures and morale and if there was anything in her opinion that was a concern. In no way did he sound condescending or patronizing, only honestly concerned. Immediately her apprehension about working for him dropped. She was just starting to explain how they arranged the vacation schedule when their food came.

Molly stared down at her plate. Even though she hadn't been a Christian long, the pastor's sermon on remembering Jesus every time you ate and drank had really hit home. It had been a sermon meant for communion, but she'd taken it very much to heart for every day. The trouble was, she'd hadn't been in a public restaurant since she made her decision except for once after church with the church crowd. She didn't know what to do, especially with a stranger.

∞

Ken glanced down at his plate, then back up at Molly. He hated moments like this. He'd never been shy about pausing for a word of thanks before eating in a public restaurant, but he was usually with people he knew. He didn't want to look overbearing, and even worse, he didn't want to embarrass

Molly, or himself, for that matter. He deliberately kept prayers before a meal short, but when he lunched with a client or associate who wasn't a believer, he only closed his eyes for a second or two in order to be as discreet as possible, then carried on with the business at hand. He didn't like to do that, but it looked like this would be one of those times.

Across the table from him, Molly seemed to be studying her plate. As far as he could see, everything looked fine, and as far as he could remember, it was what she ordered, what she claimed was her favorite house special. Since she wasn't paying any attention to him, he decided it would be a good time to close his eyes briefly when Molly closed her eyes, bowed her head, and clasped her hands on the tabletop in front of her.

His heart caught in his throat at the realization of what she was doing. He'd seen more subtle ways for someone in doubt of their surroundings to pause for a word of grace, but with that hair, he doubted anything this woman did could be subtle.

"Molly?"

Her eyes opened and her cheeks reddened.

"Would you mind if I said grace?"

The change from her open mouth and red face to her beaming smile almost made him feel lightheaded.

"I'd love that!"

A few people briefly turned their heads at her sudden exclamation. Quickly, Ken composed himself, bowed his head, closed his eyes, and folded his hands in his lap under the table. "Dear Lord, thank You for the food You've given us, and the day before us. Thank You for Your kindness and mercy, and for Your blessings in the days to come. Amen."

He picked up his fork, prepared to start eating, but couldn't with Molly staring at him.

"Yes?"

She turned her head from side to side, checking to see if they were being watched or if anyone around them was listening. "You're a Christian!" she said in a loud whisper.

"Yes."

"For how long?"

Ken narrowed one eye. This was not a question he'd been asked before. Everyone he knew didn't have to ask. "Since I was seven years old."

Her eyes opened wide with wonder, she grasped the edge of the table with both hands and leaned forward. "Wow. . . ," she murmured.

The brilliant green of her eyes drew him like a magnet. He felt like an idiot, staring at each other across the table while their food cooled, but he couldn't look away.

It was almost like another person was asking, but Ken heard his own voice. "How about you?"

She sat back in her chair and smiled. "A week ago last Wednesday!"

He'd never spoken to a new believer before, at least not that he knew of. He didn't know what to say, so he said nothing.

"So where do you go to church?"

"I just arrived in Vancouver this morning, so nowhere, yet."

"Have you ever been to Vancouver before?"

"A couple of times."

"It hardly ever snows in the winter here. Some years it doesn't snow at all. I hear Winnipeg gets tons of snow, I couldn't imagine what it would be like. It really doesn't rain in Vancouver as much as people say it does, and there's so much to see and do. Have you ever been to Science World? It's not just for kids, they have. . ." Her voice trailed off and her smile dropped. "Sorry, I think you'd asked me about vacation scheduling."

Ken tried not to shake his head. *Vacation scheduling? Was that today?*

He listened politely as a very subdued Molly explained more about day-to-day happenings in the office, and before he knew it, their lunches were done and they were back at work.

For most of the afternoon, he spent his time in the accounting department going over their larger client's transaction histories, but out of the corner of his eye, he watched Molly diligently piling and sorting old and dated files, then placing them into boxes once they were in order.

At the end of the day, everyone filed out, except for Molly. Nancy, the accounting department supervisor, offered to stay but Ken sent her home as well. Even Uncle Walter left, leaving himself and Molly the only ones remaining in the building.

Ken walked to the desk as she dropped the last file into a box. "You can go home, Molly. I don't want you to stay on my account."

She shook her head. "No, it took me all day to get these sorted, I don't want to stop now. I got everything put away in the main storage room, all that I've got left is what goes in the attic. It should only take me an hour, and then I won't have it hanging over my head. This way we can get a fresh start tomorrow. I don't mind."

"Well, then I'll help you, and together we'll do it in half the time."

≥▲

Molly fumbled with the box in her hands, and let it drop with a thump on the desktop.

She never did get her errands done at lunchtime. Since it was Friday night, she'd been invited to go play volleyball with the young adult group at church. She'd resigned herself to not being able to go in order to do what she had to, since she'd given up her lunch break to talk to Ken. If this was a way to get finished quicker, then perhaps she would still be able to participate.

She raised her eyes. All she could do was stare at him as he stood before her, waiting for her to say something. Ken Quinlan wasn't here to do filing. Obviously he was being set up for a supervisory or management position, most likely in accounting. No doubt his presence had something to do with the rumors that were floating around. Even though she didn't know what the long range plans were, word was this move was permanent.

"You? You're going to put stuff away in the dark, dusty storage room?"

He shrugged his shoulders and gave her a grin that made her breath catch. "Why not? Unless you don't want my help."

"You know this isn't just carrying these boxes and leaving them there. I have to take out every single file, pull out whichever box they belong in, one at a time, and put them all away."

"I know how archived files are stored, Molly. We're required to keep files for seven years. They have to go somewhere."

Molly looked at his suit, which probably cost as much as her entire wardrobe. "If you have asthma or dust allergies, you'll never survive up there. Do you have any idea how dirty it is in the attic? And you'll ruin your suit."

"Well, there's only one way to solve that." With that statement, Molly stared as Ken removed his suit jacket and slung it over the back of his chair, then loosened and pulled off his hand-painted silk tie and laid it over the jacket. Next, he rolled up his sleeves and picked up one of the larger boxes. "Lead the way."

two

Who was she to argue? After all, Ken was now the boss.

Molly snuck a peek at him as he lifted the largest box and settled it securely in his muscular arms. Even minus the suit jacket and tie, he was still every inch a professional. A five-o'clock shadow darkened his jaw, making her wonder how long he'd been awake, especially considering his early morning flight and the time-zone change. She tried to be as discreet as possible as she scanned his masculine features. Despite signs of fatigue, he continued on.

She was aware of his every footstep behind her as they walked through the office and up the back stairs to the storage room in the attic.

Molly groped around the corner for the switch and flicked it on, cringing at the layer of dust beneath her fingertips. The single bare bulb barely lit the room, which was probably a blessing in disguise, because the dim light didn't allow a complete picture of the thick dust and grime. The few occasions she'd spent any amount of time here, Molly had brought a change of clothing and a kerchief to cover her hair. This area was cleaned once a year whether it needed it or not, and she suspected it was more than a little overdue this year.

Molly pushed the stool with her foot rather than touch it, leaving a circle on the floor where the dust wasn't quite as high. When she stepped up, she looked down to see a trail of her own footsteps and wondered what the dirt would do to Ken's imported patent leather shoes.

But the sooner she started, the sooner she would be home. She turned and stood on her tiptoes atop the stool to reach the "N" box for 1994.

"I can do that, Molly."

"It's okay," she mumbled between her teeth as she pulled out the dust covered box. She knew her functional dress would launder better than his silk shirt and expensive slacks for his tailor-made suit. They would both get dirty, but this way he would get less dirty than she would. "I think it will work better if I find the boxes, since I know where most of them are, I'll hand them to you; you put the file away and hand the box back to me."

She took his silence for agreement and handed him the first dirty box. He opened it, inserted the file, and returned it, and Molly slid it back. They continued in silence, slowly working their way down the shelving unit, until they were at the corner next to the stair opening.

Molly slid the stool to the corner, located the next box she needed, and pulled, but it was stuck. She pulled harder, but still it didn't move.

"Let me try that. I'm taller than you, I can maneuver it easier."

"No," she mumbled between her teeth as she pulled harder, "I think I've got it. It's just—" The aged cardboard ripped, and with the release of tension, Molly's whole body jerked backward. With the piece of torn cardboard still in her hand, she flailed her arms but couldn't regain her balance. The stool shot out from beneath her feet, and Molly toppled backward.

"Molly!" Ken shouted behind her.

His hands touched her back at the same time as she tumbled down. They grunted in unison as she thumped against him then crashed into the doorframe together. A sharp bump at the small of her back propelled her slightly forward before she crumpled to the ground at the same time as a sickening crash echoed on the stairs behind her.

Molly tried to scramble to her feet, but her skirt caught on the metal shelving unit. When she started to push herself up, her shoe slid in the layer of dust and the pull of the skirt held her in place. She yanked her skirt, not caring about the sound of ripping fabric, and clambered toward the stairs, where Ken lay, arms and legs splayed.

Molly's heart pounded as she wondered if she should touch him, and if she did, should she try to move him or feel for a pulse.

Before she reached him he moved one arm, started to push himself up, then groaned and sank down again. She scrambled down three steps, plopped her bottom down on the stair and helped pull him up by the shoulders until he was at a sitting position, leaning against the metal stair railing. His teeth were tightly clenched and his eyes squeezed shut, all the color drained from his face.

"Ken! Ken! Say something! Are you all right!?"

He clutched his arm tightly, and slowly his eyes opened. His words came out slow and strained. "I don't know."

❧

"You did WHAT!?"

Molly lowered her head and buried her face in her hands. The bright and cheerful music from the worship team at the front of the sanctuary did little to lift her sagging spirits. "I said, I nearly killed my boss's favorite relative."

Robbie's hand rested gently on Molly's shoulder while her husband, Garrett, snickered behind her. She heard a muffled *oomph*, and Garrett was silent.

"Come on, Molly," Robbie said in a sympathetic whisper. "What really happened?"

Molly shook her head without removing her hands from her face. "I'm serious. He was going to help me put some old files away, and I knocked him down the stairs, and he broke his arm, and it's all my fault. And he was such a nice guy."

"Molly, he's not dead, I'm sure he still *is* a nice guy. And bones heal."

"I know he'll heal, but tomorrow morning they're going to fire me. I should wear my pajamas to work, because they're just going to send me right back home again."

Garrett's deep voice sounded from behind Robbie, but Molly couldn't look at him as he spoke. "They won't fire you, it was an accident. Accidents happen, Robbie should know. Right, Robbie?"

"Never mind," Robbie mumbled. Garrett grunted again and stayed silent. Robbie's voice brightened. "The service is about to begin, but we'll pray for you. And him, too. What's his name?"

Molly finally looked up at her friends at the exact second the volume of the music lowered, the overhead lights dimmed, and the screen with the music words lit up. The worship leader's voice boomed a welcome to the congregation over the PA system.

"His name is Ken."

❧

Ken squirmed in his seat, barely paying attention. The organist played a somber hymn at a low volume while the minister read a few highlights from the bulletin. His arm still hurt, but at least his wrist wasn't throbbing quite as bad as it was yesterday. He'd woken up yesterday in a daze, waiting for the effects of the bad dream to pass. Instead, reality set in. The pain didn't stop. It had really happened.

Every motion he made on the hard wooden pew irritated the massive bruise on his back, and the support strap of the sling dug into his neck. Again, he shifted to sit straight to stop compensating against the unnatural lean to support the weight of the cast.

He peeked to follow from Aunt Ellen's hymnal as they started singing. He certainly wasn't going to make any attempt to hold anything until the swelling in his fingers subsided, which they told him would be about a week. The doctor at the emergency department told him he had been lucky to get away with "only" a broken arm, a slight fracture in his wrist, a few sprained fingers, and a lot of bruising. His shoulder hadn't been dislocated, it was "only" a pulled ligament. He really didn't feel so lucky. He hurt all over.

He still couldn't believe what had happened. When he woke up Saturday morning he'd almost convinced himself it had been a bad dream, until he tried to move, and this morning wasn't much better. The only thing that made all the pain and inconvenience worthwhile was that he'd been able to prevent Molly from falling down the stairs and breaking her neck.

Molly.

Miss Molly McNeil was really something. Uncle Walter had said he had the perfect employee to show him general procedures from the ground up. Of course, he hadn't taken that to literally mean from the bottom of a stairwell. He smiled to himself, then quickly lowered his head, winced at the kink in his neck, and stared at the hymnal once again before anyone noticed that his mind was elsewhere.

He liked her. He liked her outspoken spirit, her dedicated work ethic, and the way she carried herself. And she was a believer. Despite her junior position in the corporate structure, she made great efforts to do her best, to know her job, and pay attention to what went on around her. It made her a valuable asset to the company, at least in his eyes. First impressions were important in the professional world, and every time he'd phoned through from the Winnipeg office he'd thought highly of the way the receptionist handled his calls. And now he'd finally met her in person.

He even liked her fiery red hair. Not that she was his type, but if she wasn't an employee, he might have tried to get to know her better. After Molly had dropped him off at his aunt and uncle's home Friday night following his visit at the hospital and when Aunt Ellen finished fussing with his injuries, he'd asked about her. Uncle Walter didn't know Molly was a Christian, and therefore had no idea what church she attended, but Ken could plainly see she didn't attend this one. He could have picked her hair out of any crowd from a mile away.

The congregation stood, the movement causing him to focus his thoughts on where they should have been in the first place. However, when the worship time was finished and the congregation bowed their heads, Ken's prayers drifted to Molly McNeil, asking God to hold her up, because he knew she felt terrible about what had happened.

Despite what he'd already discovered to be a quick tongue, she possessed a kind heart. She'd been very upset at the hospital, and a number of times throughout the examination and steps to set the break and fit the cast he thought she was going to break into tears. He'd tried to assure her it wasn't her fault, but he knew he hadn't convinced her.

He could hardly wait until work tomorrow, when he would see her again. It would be easier to talk to her after a few days since it happened and emotions weren't running so rampant.

❧

Molly deliberately drove extra slow on her way to work. She had only been joking when she told Robbie she would wear her pajamas to work, but she hadn't been joking about the likelihood of getting fired.

When she drove Ken to Mr. Quinlan's home after the hospital, the scene she witnessed showed her that Mr. and Mrs. Quinlan loved Ken like the son they never had. Not much had been said except for fussing over poor Ken, although they'd assured her they knew it was only an accident. But, after the shock of seeing him with his dirty and battered clothes and the cast on his arm wore off, she wondered if Mr. Quinlan would have second thoughts.

She buried her face in her hands as she waited for a red light. A million things could have happened. He could have broken his neck and ended up in a wheelchair. Or he could have been killed. For the millionth time, she praised God that compared to the possibilities, he was relatively fine.

Still, it was all her fault. She was responsible. She wanted to make it up to him, but first she had to face him.

A car horn behind her jolted her to attention, and she took off with a screech of rubber.

As she passed a florist, she wondered if maybe she should stop and buy flowers or something, although some things were beyond an apology. Men bought flowers for women all the time to express what words could not. But she drove on, not wanting it to look like she was sniveling, even though she would have done so if it could have made things better.

Reluctantly, Molly pulled into her parking space and dragged her feet all the way in the front door of the gaping office tower. A couple of the sales staff stood talking in the lobby as she opened the door. Conversation instantly stopped as they artlessly stared at her as she entered.

Molly kept walking.

She continued through the foyer and into the open area of the main office. As soon as people saw her, a collective hush grew.

Molly wished she could melt into the cracks in the floor. She kept her sights focused straight ahead as she walked to her new desk.

"Molly? Could I see you for a minute in private, please?"

Molly cringed. Ken stood in the doorway of Mr. Quinlan's office. He wore a suit, but the left sleeve hung empty. At waist height, his still reddened and puffy fingers stuck out from the white cast beneath the jacket. He smiled, but the effect was completely negated by the dark circles under his eyes.

As she approached, Mr. Quinlan rose and left the office

People started whispering. Molly forced herself to breathe and concentrated on every step she took.

She followed Ken inside, and he closed the door. Instead of sitting in Mr. Quinlan's chair, he sat in the same chair he'd sat in on Friday and nodded for her to sit as well.

"Hi, Molly."

"Hi," she choked out. "How are you?" Molly bit her lip at the inaneness of her question.

"I'm okay. It still hurts, of course, but I'll heal. I wanted to assure you that neither myself nor Uncle Walter hold you in any way responsible. It was an accident."

Molly felt her throat tighten. "But it was my fault, and I'm so sorry. I don't know what to say or do, but I've been think-ing of you all weekend. And I seem to remember a little push just before you fell down the stairs. You pushed me away so I wouldn't fall down the stairs, but that made you fall down instead of me. I don't know how I can ever thank you."

ᘒ

Ken forced himself to smile. The last thing he wanted was her gratitude, but her recollection of that split second was accurate. He wouldn't have mentioned it, but since she did, she forced him to deal with it. "I don't want your thanks. But I'll tell you what I do want. It seems I'm going to need more help than I originally planned. Instead of just a week, I'd like you to be my personal assistant until I'm out of the cast."

Her face paled. "Me? After all this?"

"It's not your fault, Molly. Really. And yes, you."

Her eyes trailed down to his throbbing fingers, tightly encased in the plaster cast, then back up to his face. He held himself stiffly, avoiding attempting to analyze why it was so important she agreed.

"Of course I'll help. It's the least I can do. If you can trust me."

"If I didn't trust you, I wouldn't have asked."

Her voice trembled. "Thank you."

Ken stood, very pleased with the way things were turning out. "This afternoon I'll have you type up a few letters for me. Normally I would just type them myself on the com-puter, but I'm obviously not going to be typing for a while."

Molly stood in front of him. "Yes, well. . ." She looked down at his arm again. The jacket had slipped back on his shoulder, exposing more of the cast, which due to the nature of the break, encompassed his wrist and extended past his elbow, part way up his upper arm. "At least it's your left arm."

He didn't want to tell her, but he knew it would come up soon or later. "I'm left handed."

She stared at his swollen and aching fingers, then covered her face with her hands. "Oh, no. . ."

three

As she slowly lifted her head, their gazes locked. She blinked rapidly a few times, her lower lip quivered, her eyes became glassy, then watery, and one lone tear slid down her cheek. "I'm so sorry. . . ."

Ken couldn't stop himself. He knew he shouldn't touch her, especially if there was the slightest chance that any of the staff could see through the mini-blinds of his uncle's office, but he did it anyway. He lifted his right hand, gently resting his fingertips on her cheek, and brushed the tear away with the pad of his thumb. Another one followed.

Ken felt like he'd just been dealt a sucker-punch to his gut. He'd never let tears affect him, but he had no doubt of Molly's sincerity.

"Don't worry, Molly. I'll heal. We can make the best of it."

❧

Molly nodded, stiffened her back, and clasped her hands in front of her. She was going to get herself under control, walk to her new desk, and begin her new duties. She trusted Ken when he said neither he nor his uncle held the accident against her, and she'd never been more thankful for anything in her life, except, of course, that Ken wasn't seriously hurt.

Briefly, Ken outlined his schedule for the day, giving Molly some instructions, and she left to begin her new duties. Ken remained inside the office until Mr. Quinlan returned, and they shut the door.

Everyone was watching her. She could feel it. Her first impulse was to stand up and yell out that it was an accident and for everyone to mind their own business, but these people were not only her workmates, some of them were her friends. Also, being a Christian, she wanted to show everyone Christ's

24

love and that she was grateful for the forgiveness offered her, which meant she shouldn't snap at them for their understandable curiosity.

While she doubted Mr. Quinlan had made an announcement about the circumstances concerning poor Ken's broken arm, she knew that in every organization there was always someone who discovered details which should have been considered private. She couldn't figure out who in this case might have found out she'd been the cause, but she could tell from the second she walked in the door that everyone already knew.

Molly purposely kept her head down, and since she successfully managed to ignore everyone around her, they eventually started to ignore her and carry about their own business.

Unfortunately, coffee break came too soon. She accompanied the usual group into the lunchroom, and the second she sat down, she was surrounded.

"How did you do it?"

"What were you really doing up there in the storage room?"

"How mad was he?"

"How come Mr. Quinlan didn't fire you?"

"What's he like?"

Molly plunked her mug down, not caring that some coffee sloshed out, and buried her face in her hands. "It was an accident," she mumbled. She'd already embarrassed herself by crying in front of Ken, but at the onslaught of questions, she felt on the verge of tears again. She didn't want to cry in front of everyone. Things were bad enough already.

"Come on, you guys, leave her alone. Can't you tell she's upset about it? How would you feel if you broke the boss's arm?"

Molly peeked through her fingers to see Janice shooing everyone away.

Janice. Whom Molly had hated for a while yesterday when she thought Janice stole her job, even though it wouldn't have been Janice's fault. The force of the guilt hit her right smack between the eyes. She knew there had to be a Bible verse for that somewhere. Tonight, she would ask Robbie, but as soon as she regained control of herself, this could be a great chance to witness to Janice. The sermon yesterday had focused on being a good Christian example, which was necessary to help spread the word of God's gift of salvation. Molly could see she was going to learn a lot on Sunday mornings. This would be a good chance to share her faith and show God how thankful she was for Jesus, her Savior.

For lack of something more dignified to do with her hands, Molly lowered her hands to steady them on her coffee mug, blinked away the sting of pending tears, and forced herself to smile. "Thank you, Janice."

Janice simply shrugged her shoulders.

Molly opened her mouth, but she couldn't think of the right opening for sharing her faith, short of blurting out something out of context, which would destroy her credibility. Pastor Harry had said the greatest tool in witnessing to the unsaved was friendship and earning the right to be heard. So, instead, they chatted amicably until it was time to return to work, but that didn't stop Molly from inserting a few references to attending church into the conversation.

On her way out, Molly poured herself another coffee, then paused. She knew Ken was a coffee drinker and highly suspected he didn't want to attempt to pour it with the wrong hand, nor would he ask anyone to do it for him. Therefore, Molly selected a spare mug from the cupboard and poured him a fresh cup, adding cream and one spoon of sugar, just like she remembered from their lunch together.

By the time she returned, Ken was busy pecking at his computer with one finger and muttering under his breath. His suit jacket lay draped sloppily across the back of his chair, giving more prominence to the white sling and the reason for his frustration.

She placed her mug on her desk, then stood beside him

with the other steaming mug in her hand. "Hi. I brought you a coffee. I thought you could probably use one."

His hand froze above the keyboard. He sighed and turned his head to look up at her. His bleak expression caused her hand to tremble as she slowly lowered the mug to an empty spot on the desk.

"Thanks. I'm glad you're here. This is much harder than I thought it would be."

"I guess you're probably having a hard time typing. Sometimes I try and use one hand to type while I'm eating a sandwich, and it doesn't work very well." She covered her mouth with her hands. "Oops! We're not supposed to eat at the computers. Crumbs and stuff, you know. You won't tell Mr. Quin. . .uh. . .your uncle, will you?"

He grinned, but the smile didn't reach his eyes. "As long as you don't tell when I do it."

Molly smiled back. She had the feeling she was going to like working with him.

Ken leaned back in his chair and ran his fingers through his hair. "Typing is bad enough, but the mouse is driving me nuts."

"The mouse?" Molly picked up his mouse and shook it. "What's wrong with it? This mouse is new."

He sighed again. "It's so awkward with my right hand."

"Working a mouse is easy. How hard could it be, even with the other hand?"

"Have you ever tried to work a mouse with your left hand?"

"Well, no. . ."

Ken shoved the keyboard to the side, picked up the mousepad, and placed it on the left side of the keyboard, stood, and stepped aside. "Be my guest."

Molly stared into his face and tried not to let her mouth hang open. Even though she hadn't known him long, the change in him was a shock to her system. Gone was the softness in his face she'd witnessed a few minutes ago, replaced by tight lines on his brow and the hardening of his lips. He stretched out his free arm with an abrupt movement, signaling her to sit in his chair.

Molly lowered her gaze as she studied the mouse, still in her hand. Fortunately no one in the vicinity had noticed their stalemate, so Molly sat before anyone did notice. Switching the mouse into her left hand, she began to guide it onto the program he had open.

"This isn't hard."

"Okay, open the Brentwood file."

Carefully, Molly aimed the mouse, ran it down the list, and then clicked. Nothing happened. "Oops, I used the wrong button. They seem to be reversed for the wrong hand." Her words caught in her throat. "I didn't mean the wrong hand. I meant the left hand."

Her comment was met with silence.

She slid the mouse to the list again, but the arrow went in the wrong direction.

"Oops."

Working very slowly, she guided the mouse to the correct entry and tried to stop it from wiggling when she used her ring finger instead of her index finger to click with the left mouse button.

Finally it worked.

"Now open their financial file."

She didn't know if she wanted to go through it again. "I think you've proved your point. I'm sorry, Ken. I really haven't thought about how right handed the world is. The keyboard even has the calculator part on the right side. I'll bet back home you have one of those ones that splits, and you can move it to the left, don't you?"

"Yes, I do. I've ordered a new one, but it hasn't come yet. Not that there's a rush now. I won't be able to use it for six to eight weeks."

Molly cringed. At that moment she made up her mind to attempt some basic tasks using her left hand, just so she'd remember how difficult this was going to be for him. She didn't know much about stuff designed for lefties, but she did know there were special scissors and that baseball mitts for left handed people were twice the price of the regular ones. Of course that didn't matter for now. He couldn't use his left hand if he wanted to.

"Would you mind entering this information and then add up this spreadsheet for me?"

She nearly made a comment about gladly doing all his menial tasks and that he didn't have to ask since his situation was her fault, but Molly bit her tongue. Despite his frustration, Ken was being far more gracious than she would have been, and she didn't want to push her luck.

She only knew two people who were raised in a Christian home, her friend Gwen and Gwen's brother Garrett, whom she'd been seeing much more often lately since Garrett married her best friend, Robbie. If this was typically the way a person who was raised in a Christian home behaved, she decided to learn from his example. She considered cornering Ken with her growing list of questions, rather than waiting until Bible Study night, when she could ask Gwen and Garrett.

She switched the mouse back to the right side, saved the file to a disk, piled up Ken's spreadsheets, and returned to her own desk.

She was nearly finished when Ken's voice beside her made her jump.

"Are you busy for lunch?"

Molly's fingers froze midsentence. Work and conversation around them stopped.

The errands she'd planned for her lunch break on Friday were still not completed. Instead of doing them on the weekend, she'd spent most of her time moping around and feeling sorry for herself. Rather than looking up, she stared at her fingers, which she held motionless over the keyboard. This whole situation was her fault. She couldn't turn down anything he asked.

Molly looked up. "I guess not."

He smiled, and she immediately knew she'd done the right thing. "Great. Where should we go?"

Since doing her errands would take too long to meet him at the restaurant after and dragging him around with her while she picked up her photographs and dry cleaning was out of the question, her errands would have to wait.

Still sitting in the chair as he stood beside her, his poor swollen fingers at eye level reminded her that everything he did had to be accomplished with one hand. Unless she was also expected to cut up his food, their choices were limited. She doubted he would be able to eat a sloppy burger with one hand, and there was a great Chinese place around the corner, but she didn't think he'd be able to manage chopsticks with the wrong hand. She could barely manage them with her right one.

"Why don't we go to the same place as last time? They have great ravioli."

"Sure. Let's go now and beat the rush."

Beating the rush was never an option before, but being the boss's relative gave one privileges that lowly office staff like her could only dream of. Molly hit save and stood. "Sure. I'll go bring the car out front."

"No, I'll drive this time. I haven't gone out to buy a car yet, but I can borrow my uncle's."

She opened her mouth to protest but snapped it shut quickly. Who was she to argue?

With a quick nod, he stood aside, then Molly followed him to the underground parking. He hadn't made a special trip to get the keys, proving he already had this planned. She chose to ignore everyone staring as they left.

Slowly, he backed the large car out of the narrow stall so Molly could open the door. She didn't like big cars, which made her wonder what kind of car Ken had. Not that she should care.

Ken waited for her to fasten her seatbelt before he exited the parking lot. "You'll have to give me directions. I don't think I can drive through the short cuts like when we walked."

Molly pointed to the right. "Two blocks that way, then one block left. How are you going to get your car here? Is someone going to drive it out for you?"

He shook his head. "I sold it. I was going to buy something new once I got here. I just haven't yet."

She noticed he was too nice to say it was because he wasn't in any shape to go looking over the weekend. She also had a niggling suspicion that the major reason was that he couldn't sign the registration papers for the car or the other legal forms for transferring his drivers license. She said nothing.

"I was also going to look around for a house once I got here, too, but since my stuff is all in storage anyway, Uncle Walter and Aunt Ellen insisted I stay with them until I'm out of the cast."

Molly cringed. Something else that was her fault.

Once they were seated and their orders had been taken, Ken's expression turned serious. "I'm afraid we're going to have to discuss business. I was tied up all morning, and there's a big meeting first thing this afternoon, so this is all the free time I had. I hope you don't mind."

She was quickly coming to understand how Ken was moving rapidly up the corporate ladder. Even temporarily handicapped, he carried himself in a style Molly couldn't quite put her finger on, but left no question as to his authority, despite his age. His manners were impeccable, his words gentle but firm. He left no question of who was in charge.

"Tell me about Trevor Chapman. So far all I've learned is from his corporate file, the status of their account, their needs, but nothing about what the man is like to do business with, his preferences and concerns. As receptionist, you speak frequently to all our clients, big and small, including Mr. Chapman."

Now she was starting to realize why she had been chosen to assist him. Not that she had been involved in sales, but she did have a lot of contact with all their business associates, even if it wasn't for the specialized dealings of day to day operations.

As best she could, she told him about Trevor Chapman, how everyone always jumped through hoops for him, that he expected everything immediately if not sooner, and was rather impatient if it didn't happen that way. And also that Trevor Chapman was allergic to his granddaughter's new Pekinese puppy, whom the little girl had thoughtfully named Missykins.

Ken stared blankly at Molly, trying to figure out how she knew that. What little he did know was that the man traveled only in very small and elite circles. "You know the man personally?"

Molly laughed and waved one hand in front of her mouth as she finished her bite. "Me? Of course not. Sometimes I chat with people when they're on hold and I don't have another call coming in."

Ken blinked and continued to watch Molly. Chatting was one thing, but he failed to see how a business client's granddaughter's puppy and his medical history could possibly enter a conversation.

"You know, someone really ought to change that music over the phone line when people are put on hold. It's really bad."

Ken had never paid attention to the music. He tended to ignore it while he worked on something else while waiting.

She didn't wait for his response before she started again. "I have a friend who's got a great collection of Christian CD's. It sure would be nice if we could put one of those on instead of that elevator-musak. But I guess we can't do that, can we?"

He raised one eyebrow but said nothing. Molly's face reddened, which Ken thought quite amusing.

"Oops. It was only a suggestion. Forget it. It probably wouldn't work."

He'd never even remotely considered putting Christian music over the company telephone system.

"Since you've been a Christian since you were a little kid,

I'll bet you've got a great CD collection, too, don't you?"

He was beginning to wonder when he was going to get a chance to speak. "Most of my CD's are packed in a box in storage. But you're welcome to go through the few I brought. They're in a box at my Uncle Walter's house."

"I still have a box I haven't unpacked, and I've been in my apartment for three years."

Ken shook his head. He thought they were going to talk about Trevor Chapman's company, but he'd obviously been wrong, although he wasn't quite sure what they had talked about.

Soon they were back in the car and on their way. He turned south and checked the dashboard clock. They had plenty of time.

"Ken? Where are you going?"

Fortunately, Ken had a good memory for numbers. He'd memorized the address before they left for lunch. "I already told you. We have a meeting with Trevor Chapman and his associates."

Molly's face paled. "We?"

four

They rode in silence to the highrise in the middle of the downtown core and entered the massive underground parking lot. Ken pocketed the keys, wiggled one arm into the sleeve of his suit jacket, and draped the other side as best he could over his left shoulder, then they started walking through the lot.

"You never told me I'd be going to a big meeting today. Look at what I'm wearing!" Molly pressed the button to summon the elevator.

Ken stood back and analyzed what she deemed inappropriate. She wore a black blouse accompanied by a loose skirt that was some indescribable strange shade of green, along with hose and shoes that matched the skirt. Compared to her vivid hair, her outfit was subtle and controlled, and he liked it. As he assessed the combination once more, his breath caught. The skirt was the exact color of her eyes. Those wide, gorgeous eyes. Laughing eyes, eyes that hid nothing, a gateway to her soul. Eyes a man could get lost in, perhaps for a lifetime.

Ken cleared his throat, lifted his free hand to his tie, wiggled it, then let his hand drop. "You look nice."

The light indicated the elevator was on the way down, so they patiently waited.

"I don't do shorthand or anything like that. I don't know why you need me to come with you."

His experienced secretary back in the Winnipeg office hadn't done shorthand either. Without knowing for sure, he was almost positive that such a skill was a lost art. "I know you don't. I just need someone to take notes for me."

Molly opened her mouth, her gaze dropping to his fingers

34

sticking out from the confines of the cast. Her mouth opened then snapped shut, and all the sparkle left her eyes. He had tried his best to be gentle with his words, but facts were facts. He couldn't write.

"This is a really important meeting, isn't it?"

He nodded and felt the knot of his tie again. Not only was it their largest client, Trevor Chapman was a powerful influence in the business community, and his recommendation would go far to obtain new clients or shake up current ones. This was also Ken's first time representing Quinlan Enterprises in his new capacity, even though it hadn't become official yet. Much to his relief, he and Uncle Walter had decided they would wait until he was out of the cast before making the official announcement.

Molly, the reason for his cast, flinched when the bell sounded, indicating the elevator had arrived. After a few people exited, Ken waited for Molly to precede him. Instead, she waited for him to go first.

Automatically, he began to move his left arm to gesture to Molly to go first, but the weight of the cast and twinge in his shoulder made him wince. He found it difficult to make a conscious decision to make previously automatic gestures with his right hand and wondered how long it would be before he would get used to doing these things with the wrong arm. He could also foresee that when this whole thing was over, he would be doing a lot less talking with his hands.

Molly finally started to step forward, but since they took so long to move, the door started to close. Before he thought to use his right arm, Molly beat him to it, gave the door a push, and held it open for him.

Ken stiffened. He was still old-fashioned enough to hold a door open for a lady, and to have a lady hold the elevator open for him didn't sit right.

Once inside, she released the door, and it began to close. He carefully aimed one finger at the button for the top floor and pushed. He didn't get it dead center, but he did hit the correct button. Fortunately left-handed people were more adept at using their right hand than right-handed people were at using their left. When he turned, Molly stepped closer to him.

For a moment, they stood in complete silence. Molly cleared her throat. "Your tie is crooked. I didn't want to say anything in front of anyone."

Ken smiled. He couldn't tell if it was straight without using both hands and admired Molly's discretion. He started to raise his free hand to do the best he could to fix it under the circumstances but stopped when Molly spoke.

"Let me do it for you. It looked like it bugged you, earlier. You'll never get it straight by yourself with only one. . . Uh, I mean, without a mirror."

Molly stepped exactly in front of him and raised her hands. Ken drew in a deep breath, then forced himself to relax when she touched him. This morning, Aunt Ellen had helped him with his tie, but it didn't feel like this. Molly's gentle touch seemed personal, even though he knew that wasn't her intent. He looked down, willing her to make eye contact, but instead, all her concentration remained fixed on his tie. She diligently gave it a gentle tug, wiggled it with both hands, then gave it a pat. He tried to justify the odd sensation in his chest to the motion as the elevator started to rise.

"There you go." She stepped back as a ringing telephone broke the silence. "You'd better answer your cell phone."

"I don't have my cell phone with me. I still have to obtain a local number and get it connected."

They both turned to stare at the closed compartment containing the emergency telephone. A second ring confirmed their suspicions.

Ken scrinched his eyebrows. "I've never heard one of those things ring before. How about that?"

Molly nodded. "Me neither. What do you think we should do?"

"Do? Nothing."

Molly glanced from side to side, then pulled the little door open. "I have to answer it. What if it's an emergency?"

"That's impossible. That phone is meant to be used for people who might be trapped in the elevator to call out, not for anyone to call in."

"Well, maybe there's something wrong at the top, and someone has to tell us something."

"I don't think so. I think—"

"Hello?"

Ken cringed. She'd actually answered it.

She laughed. "No, you've got the wrong number. There's no one here by that name."

He sighed, waiting for her to hang up, but instead she shook her head and touched her finger to the body of the phone.

"You've got the wrong number. I mean yes, that's the number you dialed, but you won't believe this. The number you called is inside an elevator."

Molly laughed and nodded. "Yes, I'm very serious."

The elevator continued to rise. Ken looked up to the number display above the door. They were half way to the top floor. "Say good-bye and hang up, Molly," he said quietly.

She shook her head at him while she continued to listen to the caller. Fortunately the elevator was still moving upward. Chatting with a client on the office phone was one thing, but answering the phone in an elevator?

"Yeah, this is the main elevator in the Stevens Building downtown. You know, the big brown building with the row of blue windows all the way up the side. The one beside the big trees where they had that newscast show in the spring, where they had that segment on the baby birds that hatched in the middle of busy downtown? And they ran a contest to name the baby birds?"

Ken was beginning to see how Molly had learned about their best client's personal life and medical history. "Molly. Please. Hang up," he ground out between his teeth.

"No, I never did hear who won the contest. Only it wasn't me."

The elevator slowed. "Molly. . .hang up that phone. . ."

"Really? I think those are cute names. You should have won."

The door opened. A woman and two men stepped forward, then their feet skidded to a halt just short of the entrance to the elevator.

Molly laughed. "You're kidding. That's really funny!"

The three people nervously glanced between each other, backed up a step, and the elevator door closed without anyone getting in. The elevator resumed its journey upward.

Ken glared at Molly without saying a word.

"Oops. I think I'd better go. I'm almost at my floor. Bye." She fumbled the phone as she hung up and slammed the small door closed. "Uh, it was a wrong number."

Before he could gather this thoughts, the elevator once again slowed, and the doors opened to the top floor. All he could do was stare at her.

"Don't tell me you can ignore a ringing phone!"

"If it's not my phone, yes, I can."

Molly harumphed and stomped out. "Well, I can't. Which way are we going?" She stopped short, coming to a halt so quickly Ken nearly bumped into her from behind.

Between the off-center weight of the cast and the inability to move his left arm, he couldn't regain his balance, forcing him to steady himself against the wall. He hoped no one had seen him swaying like a drunk. As he regained his balance and raised his head, Molly was staring at him.

"Ken? Are you all right? Do you want me to take you back to the office so you can lie down or something?"

Ken felt his ears heat up. "I'm fine. We're going to 2510. According to the sign, it's to the right."

&

They were welcomed into Trevor Chapman's large office and were seated in a couple of the large chairs that were arranged in a half circle in front of his desk. The door opened, and three more people entered.

It was the three people who hadn't entered the elevator.

Molly cringed, then did her best to smile when they were introduced.

She'd embarrassed Ken. She hadn't meant to, but as usual, she hadn't thought before she acted, and again, she was sorry. Molly made up her mind to sit and be completely quiet and to not speak unless spoken to.

With that thought firmly in place, the meeting progressed well, and she soon had pages and pages of notes. At the conclusion of the meeting, the other people left first. As she and Ken stood, Mr. Chapman shuffled a few objects on his desk, one of them a picture of a darling little girl holding a puppy.

Mr. Chapman beamed when Ken picked up the framed photograph to admire it. "That's my granddaughter and her new puppy."

Molly peeked over Ken's shoulder. "Oh! So that's Missy-kins! What a darling little dog." Sheepishly, Molly raised her eyes. "And your granddaughter is cute, too."

Mr. Chapman smiled like a typical proud grandpa.

"You know, I'd bet you'd like the dog better if you could get close to her without breaking out into a rash." Molly offered. "I once knew someone who was seriously allergic to dogs and cats, and he bought some over-the-counter stuff that really helped. I could phone and ask him what it was."

"It was a nonprescription remedy?"

Molly nodded. "Oh, yes, it was. It will really help if she bathes the dog before you get near it and keeps it well brushed. Did you know more people are allergic to cats than to dogs? And it's not the hair that's the allergen; it's the dander."

Out of the corner of her eye, she saw Ken squeeze his eyes shut then make a very halfhearted smile. She tried to keep smiling. Judging from his reaction, she'd done it again.

"Thank you, Miss McNeil. I'd appreciate that."

Molly pointedly checked her wristwatch. "I guess we'd better go. It was nice finally meeting you after speaking to you so often."

He simply nodded, they exchanged handshakes, and Molly and Ken left.

The second they were seated inside the car, Molly could no longer hold back. "I'm so sorry, Ken. I didn't mean to embarrass you. But you should hear him talk about his granddaughter. I know he would love to share her joy in the puppy, but he just can't get near it without feeling the effects for days. And he—"

"It's okay, Molly. You don't have to explain."

"But. . ." At the touch of his warm hand on top of her fingers, Molly let her voice trail off.

"Don't worry about it. Everything went just fine," he said evenly and started the car.

Ken retraced their route back to the office. Molly spent the trip gazing out the window, studying the tall buildings and commenting on some of the landmarks they passed, negating the need for a real conversation.

Ken had never met a woman like Molly. The first thing she thought was what came out of her mouth, which should have been a detriment. Oddly, he found the trait rather appealing, even though at the same time he feared what she might say next. She was as bold as her hair and as difficult to blend into what should have been a dignified setting. Even when her comments and observations came out of left field, she still managed to charm everyone around her. Himself included.

Ken smiled. She wasn't his type in the slightest. Bold, brassy, and once she got started, she talked a mile a minute. He preferred to stay in the background, and then take charge when he'd analyzed all components of a situation.

But he liked her anyway. He liked her too much. He'd felt a stab of something he didn't want to think about when she mentioned the male friend with the animal allergies. It gave him great satisfaction when she left the impression she no longer associated with the man. And he didn't want to think of why it was important.

five

Molly gave the dry cleaner's plastic wrapper one hefty shove into the garbage container and let the lid slam shut as she ran to catch the ringing phone.

"Hi, Molly. It's Ken. I was wondering if you were busy."

She glanced at the time. Resigned to the fact that it might be days before she could do her errands at lunchtime, she had done everything right after work, and because of that, in addition to the need to do some serious housecleaning, she hadn't eaten dinner yet.

The only reason she could think of why Ken would call her at home would be because he couldn't read the notes she made at the meeting, although she'd tried extra hard to make them legible. She didn't want to think that she'd be putting in endless hours of unpaid overtime during her allotted time as his assistant, but the guilt that his predicament was her fault nagged her. She wouldn't mind spending some extra time with him, but supper came first. She was starving.

"Well, yes actually. . ."

"Oh."

Molly's heart fluttered. He sounded disappointed. "Uh, why?"

"I was hoping you hadn't eaten yet and could join me for dinner."

Molly glanced at the freezer, where her frozen meal still was stored. She hadn't even turned the oven on yet. She ran one hand down her faded T-shirt and looked down to her ratty jeans with a hole in one knee. "I haven't had dinner yet, either, but I'm not dressed for going out. So, sorry, not this time. But you're welcome to come over later."

"How about if we order in? All you have to do is give me

your address and the directions. Just remember to talk very slowly."

"Uh, okay." She cringed, grateful he couldn't see her. She couldn't imagine trying to write with the wrong hand, but when she heard him typing the directions onto the computer as she spoke, she smiled. When she was done with the instructions, she heard him hit the print button.

As soon as she hung up, her first impulse was to change into something more presentable, but all she had time to do was to run her brush through her hair. Instead of fussing with her appearance, Molly scrambled to tidy up her apartment, which included folding her futon back into the couch, stuffing some of the clutter into her armoire, and kicking the rest under the couch.

She had just placed the last dirty glass into the dishwasher when the buzzer sounded. Ken arrived at her door with a large bag in his hand, but no briefcase. He was still wearing his suit, minus the tie. Inwardly, she cringed, wishing she had taken the few minutes to change, at least into jeans that didn't have a hole in the knee.

"You brought Chinese food? I was expecting we were going to order pizza. How are you going to eat that?"

He smiled, showing tiny crinkles at the corners of his eyes, making Molly almost forget about how hungry she was. In a way, she was relieved he'd shown up with their dinner in his hand, rather than having to wait even longer for something to be delivered.

"You don't have to eat Chinese food with chopsticks, Molly. You're allowed to use a fork. Honest."

She tried to fight it, but Molly could feel the blush in her cheeks. Instead of putting her foot even farther in her mouth, she backed up, allowing him access.

"Nice apartment. Which way is the kitchen?"

She backed up one more step. It was a small bachelor suite, which consisted of one big room—the status of which depended if she had her futon opened into a bed or folded into a couch—a kitchen, and a bathroom. "Over here." Molly pointed to her right. She could only imagine what Ken thought of her apartment in comparison to Mr. Quinlan's house, which she had seen some of when she drove him home from the hospital. Her entire apartment could fit into the Quinlan's living room. While it was small, it suited her needs and was home.

She'd already set the table, so after a short prayer of thanks, they quickly dug into the food.

"So, have you lived in Vancouver all your life? Tell me some of the interesting things to see and do here. You've already mentioned Science World."

Molly smiled. Tourists.

"They built it for Expo '86, but now the SkyTrain is part of the local transit system, as is the SeaBus. I haven't used either one a lot except for showing visitors around town, but it's quite an experience, especially if you've never been on a monorail before. "

"I've seen it going down the track on Terminal Avenue."

"I often take out-of-town friends and relatives to either Science World or the Lonsdale Quay, which is a massive marketplace, or sometimes to the Skyview Theater and Gastown on the weekend. It's a lot of fun. You can park at the Park-N-Ride, then get a one-day transit pass."

"That sounds like a nice idea. I'd like that. Is it best to go in the morning or afternoon?"

"Oh, in the morning, definitely."

"Great. Should I pick you up, or do you want to pick me up?"

Molly opened her mouth, about to tell him all about how they'd expanded the system, but the words caught in her throat. It hadn't been meant as a personal invitation, but if he'd taken it that way, she didn't want to hurt his feelings and tell him she had no intention of seeing him on the weekend. "Are you sure you want to go to a market and go riding around town?"

"Yes, planning the day like that sounds like a good introduction to living here." He smiled again, and she wondered if he knew how difficult it was to say no to him when he kept looking at her like that.

"Don't your aunt and uncle want to show you around?"

His smile never faded, and she could have sworn his eyes twinkled. "I'd rather go with you."

Molly forced herself to smile back. "Uh. . .okay. . . ." She stood and fumbled with the dirty dishes and piled them into the sink. "I guess we should go over those notes now."

Ken's smile dropped, and he blinked. "Notes?"

"You know, the notes from the meeting this afternoon."

"The notes were very comprehensive. Did you miss something? I didn't think you'd want to see them again; I left them at the office. We could go over them tomorrow if you want."

Molly stared openly at him. If he hadn't come to work, what had he come for? They hadn't talked any business so far, and since he hadn't brought what she expected, it didn't appear they were going to.

"Besides your aunt and uncle, you don't know anybody in Vancouver, do you?"

"A few people. Why?"

Molly's mind raced. *What is he doing here?* All she could do was stare at him, trying to figure him out.

"Would you mind if we moved to the couch? After sitting up in stiff office chairs all day with the weight of this cast, my back is killing me."

Rather than sit in silence, Molly turned on the television for lack of a better idea. Ken parked himself on one end of the futon, and she sat at the other. After an extended silence, the only sound in the room being some pathetic attempt at a new sitcom, Ken turned to face her.

"If you're tired, maybe I should leave."

Molly checked her watch. It was still early. "Tired? I'm not tired." She rubbed her fingers under her eyes, hoping she didn't have dark circles there. "Why do you think I'm tired?"

His answering grin quickened Molly's pulse. "You've been so quiet. I was beginning to wonder if something was wrong."

Nothing was wrong. She was still trying to figure out what he was doing there, but she couldn't come right out and ask him. In the back of her mind, the answer was that he simply wanted to be with her. The idea both flattered and terrified her.

She stared at him as he stared back at her. "Well, there is something I wanted to ask you."

A smile lit his face. "Ask away."

Her Bible sat where she'd left it on the coffee table, stuffed full of every scrap of paper she could find. She leaned forward and flipped through her many markers and opened her Bible wide open. "Right here, there's a couple of verses that I don't understand, and I'll bet you could explain them to me."

Ken's smile dropped. He cleared his throat, and his hand rose to where his tie would have been, had he been wearing one. His fingers splayed, patting the vacant spot, and his hand fell. "I'd be happy to help, if I can."

ॐ

Slowly, Molly had worked her way through all her markings and notes, stopping only briefly to bring in a snack of cookies and milk. Ken managed to answer all her questions in a manner she understood, and by the time they worked through everything, Molly appeared to be reeling with information overload.

Ken watched Molly as she closed her Bible and returned it to the coffee table beside the pile of scrap papers she'd used instead of bookmarks. While not the reason he'd come, their time had been. . .productive. But at least he'd accomplished one step in the right direction. She'd committed herself to spending a day with him. He'd taken the chance and overstepped his boundaries by fishing for an invitation, something he'd never done before. Molly had been properly polite, even though she'd been less than enthusiastic, and agreed to accompany him, for which he was tremendously relieved.

"I didn't mean to stay so late. It's nearly midnight, and we both have to get up for work in the morning."

"Uh, yeah."

She accompanied him to the door, where they stood staring at each other.

"Thanks for the invitation."

Her curious frown changed into a sly smile, the change making Ken correct his posture and want to stand closer to her. "I think you invited yourself."

He smiled back. He'd never met someone who so openly spoke aloud the first thing that ran through their mind. It was a refreshing change. "That's true. But you graciously took me up on it. Thank you."

Her face reddened. "Well, thank you for bringing supper. I was starving, and that was really good. Sure beat the frozen dinner I was going to have."

The last thing Ken wanted to do was stand at the door throwing *thank you's* back and forth like a couple of spastic parrots. What he wanted to do was. . .kiss her.

His gaze dropped to her mouth, and then he hastily returned his attention to her eyes. He liked Molly. She was different than anyone he'd ever met. She was honest and refreshing and a new believer. Unfortunately, she was also an employee. With her penchant for speaking her immediate thoughts, he could only imagine what would come out of her mouth if he did what he wanted to do or gave her any indication of what he was thinking.

He opened the door. "See you tomorrow. Good night, Molly."

❧

Ken raised his hand, about to pound his fist on the desk, then lowered it to his lap before anyone noticed. The novelty of having to do everything with the wrong hand was quickly wearing off and, unfortunately, so was the empathy people gave him along with offers of assistance.

At first he'd refused to allow his aunt to help him get dressed, but by the time he'd finally managed to at least cover all the essentials, she'd still had to do up his shirt buttons, and Uncle Walter had to tie all his ties so he could simply slip them over his head. And he would rather look less professional and not wear a belt than have anyone help him with that. As if he could grace the cover of a magazine with the cast.

He'd cut himself shaving, and resigned himself to borrowing his uncle's electric shaver, even though it didn't give as close a shave as a razor. He was sure he'd missed a few spots, but he was running so late he'd let it go. Not only did he not want to be late himself, but he nearly made his uncle late, because he had to depend on Uncle Walter for a ride. Again, Aunt Ellen had offered her car, but he didn't want to leave her stuck at home all day just because he couldn't make it out the door on time.

Briefly, Ken considered growing a beard and wearing sweatpants and a T-shirt to work. This evening he would have to go shopping, because he owned only two shirts with sleeves wide enough to fit over the cast.

The doctor had predicted that in a week he would probably regain partial use of his fingers. Their mobility would be severely hampered by the piece of cast separating his thumb, but at least he'd be able to do simple things like gel his hair himself. He felt like a little kid when Aunt Ellen gelled his hair for him. After she'd finished, it then occurred to him that he could have squeezed some gel straight onto his brush and done it that way.

He sat and stared blankly into his computer screen. The screen saver came on.

"Ken? Do you need some help?"

He turned his head and looked up. Molly stood beside him, her brows knotted as she studied him.

It wasn't her fault he couldn't aim the disk into the narrow slot on his computer properly the first time, or that he couldn't hold a pen yet. "No, thank you. This is something I have to do myself."

She shrugged her shoulders. "Well, okay then. I'm going for coffee break. Want me to bring one back for you?"

Ken stared at the pile of papers that littered his desk. He'd been struggling all day and worked through lunch to meet a deadline, and he was tired and frustrated. Despite the satisfaction it would have given him to swipe the growing stacks of paperwork into the garbage can, he neatly pushed them to the side and stood. "I think I'll go with you."

They'd almost made it to the lunchroom, when Ken thought he'd better make a detour into the washroom. The over-consumption of coffee was catching up with him, and with his limited mobility, he didn't want to embarrass himself. He swallowed his pride and asked Molly to pour his coffee for him and told her he would join her in a few minutes.

When he finally arrived at the lunchroom, Molly was sitting at a table and talking with Janice, the woman who had been temporarily assigned Molly's job as receptionist. In the two days since the switch, while Janice was doing an adequate job, he'd already heard comments that both staff and clients had missed Molly's bubbly voice on the phone.

A cup of coffee sat full and waiting for him on the table at Molly's elbow. As he approached, he couldn't help but overhear their conversation.

"Really? I've never been to church in my life. I wouldn't know what to do."

Molly smiled, causing Ken to smile as well as he continued to listen, even though it wasn't meant for him.

"I know what you mean. I've only been twice, but it's great. And already I've learned so much."

Upon his arrival, conversation stopped.

Janice stood. "I think it's time for me to get back to work. I'll talk to you later, Molly."

Ken nodded as Janice left, then sat in the chair she vacated.

He couldn't believe it. Molly had been a Christian for less than two weeks, and she was already witnessing to an unbeliever.

Guilt roared through him. He couldn't remember the last time he shared his faith outside a church setting. He tended to do his Christian service in activities amongst those already saved, or at least among those with whom most of the battle had been won and had already ventured within the church doors.

"I was beginning to wonder if you changed your mind and went back to work."

His face flamed. The convenience of wearing sweatpants to the office was less of a distant possibility. Rather than reply, he sipped the coffee.

All he could think of was Molly's efforts to speak of Christianity to Janice. If this was the typical way a new Christian behaved, with this refreshing enthusiasm and vigor, he wanted to watch her.

He'd been once to his uncle's church and knew the main core of the congregation was made up of older and well-grounded Christians. Since Molly still had lots of questions, if he could bring her to a weekly Bible study, it could serve two purposes. Molly would gain instant access to her questions in a learned and experienced atmosphere, and secondly, some of the enthusiasm of her new faith would rub off on him.

Ken smiled into his cup, hoping Molly hadn't noticed. There was also a third reason. He simply wanted to be with Molly outside of the working environment.

He sat the cup carefully on the table. "I have a question for you. Will you accompany me to Bible study tomorrow night?"

six

Molly had nearly choked on her coffee. Of all the things she guessed that could have been running through his mind at that moment, attending a Bible study would not have been one of them. As soon as the words "Me? Whatever brought that on?" left her mouth, she mentally kicked herself. Again, what she'd said to Ken came out wrong. His face flushed and his ears turned red. She'd embarrassed him and, in doing so, herself, too. Although, he was kind of cute when he blushed.

She wondered why Ken would invite her to his church's midweek Bible study but suspected that, since he really didn't know anyone yet, he probably didn't want to go alone to the house of a stranger, since he was so new in town. She never would have expected him to be shy, because he certainly wasn't shy around the office.

Robbie had invited her to a Bible study as well, and she had said she'd go, but she was sure Robbie would understand, given the reason.

When the buzzer sounded, Molly was ready. Again she wore jeans, but this time they were almost new, hemmed, and didn't have any holes. Instead of a T-shirt with a cartoon character in vivid color on the front, she had chosen a sedate long-sleeved blouse. She'd even fastened her hair back with a clip for some semblance of dignity and control. Tonight, she would be quiet and sedate. This time, she wouldn't do anything to embarrass Ken, especially in front of the people who would be his Christian family at his new church.

She stood at the door and opened it as soon as she heard the swoosh of the elevator doors. At the sight of Ken approaching, Molly nearly fainted. Instead of the prim and proper custom-tailored suits she'd become accustomed to seeing him wear, he now wore a nylon jogging outfit with a jacket made of the same fabric as the pants, and a matching T-shirt. The only thing that didn't quite match was that instead of sneakers, he wore leather shoes. And to think that she had worried about dressing too casually.

"I'm ready," she stammered.

"I've got some good news and some bad news."

Why did she not want to hear this? "Tell me the bad news first."

"The people who host the Bible study came down with the flu, so it's canceled for tonight."

"Oh." She wondered why he didn't phone to say so.

"But the good news is that the evening is now open, so you and I can do anything we want. We can have a Bible study with just the two of us, or if you'd rather go out, we can catch a show or something."

A door down the hall opened and one of her neighbors stepped out, fiddled with the lock, then very slowly headed for the elevator. She didn't feel like having her nosy neighbor listen in to their plans for the evening.

"Come in, and we'll decide on something."

He entered her apartment very quickly and pushed the door closed behind him, making Molly suspect his preference was for an invitation rather than going out. Thankfully she'd folded up her futon, just in case he came in for coffee after their Bible study was over.

"I do have a few more markers in my Bible for some stuff I was going to ask. I guess we can have a small Bible study, then. I'll make a pot of coffee."

He shook his head. "If you want coffee, that's fine, but none for me. I'm trying to cut down."

"Well, then I'll make tea instead. I'll be right back. Have a seat."

When she returned, he had already opened her Bible to the first marker, but instead of sitting on the end of the couch like last time, he parked himself right in the middle. He patted the spot beside him. "Shall we pray before we start?"

Molly nodded and slowly lowered herself beside him.

"Have you ever been to an organized Bible study?"

Molly shook her head. Ken nodded and smiled. Adorable crinkles appeared in the corners of his eyes, and the warmth of his smile did strange things to her stomach.

"What usually happens is everyone sits around and chats, and when things are ready to start, the leader will ask if there are any prayer requests or praise items."

Molly stared blankly at him. She had no idea what he was talking about.

"Oops, sorry. Let me rephrase that. Generally, everyone is asked if they have anything to tell the group. Something that they would like the group to pray for, either for themselves or a special friend or family, or, if there is something that was prayed about at a previous meeting and came to pass or just something happened where God blessed them, they might want to tell the group about it. Or if something concerns them, whether it be personal, or a world issue, like war or a natural disaster, or something they feel strongly about that they would like the group to pray about. Or even someone they know who is having difficulty and they feel led to pray about it."

"Oh."

"And often one person in the group will usually write those things down, but not always. It depends on the group."

"You're kidding. Like a journal?"

He nodded. "Exactly. It's called a prayer journal. Some people keep them for their own personal prayers, too."

"Wow. I don't think I could be organized enough to do that."

"Not everyone does that. I don't."

In a way, she found that difficult to believe.

"And then we pray. Sometimes the group will take turns, sometimes the leader will briefly mention everything that was mentioned. Again, it depends on the group."

"But that sounds so. . .organized."

"Organization is not a bad thing, Molly."

She thought of the socks and odd shoes hidden under the futon. "I guess."

The first thing she thought of was to pray for Ken and his broken arm, both for a quick healing and also for a minimum of discomfort and awkwardness while he mended. Instead, she mentioned a few family issues and then stopped.

Ken was easy to talk to, but she had to remember that he wasn't her friend, he was her supervisor. Therefore, she wasn't sure how much she should tell him or how ingrained in her life she should let him become.

She still wasn't sure what his official capacity was going to be at Quinlan Enterprises. During management meetings he contributed along with the other supervisors, and he certainly did his share of the workload and more, which was evidenced by plenty of overtime. While he was doing actual work, she could never forget that Ken Quinlan was part of the corporate family.

Talk was that he was going to be the branch manager, because he was the production manager in the plant, but no one could see that there was anything wrong with the current manager. Craig was doing a good job and ran things efficiently; his relationships with both the staff and clients were without complaint. It didn't seem the style of Quinlan Enterprises to fire someone who was doing a good job and then give the job to a relative. The trouble was, no one knew what was going on, and in the face of the unknown, rumors abounded.

Throwing caution to the wind, Molly shared a few other personal concerns. Her boss or not, she trusted him.

Scariest of all, she could actually like the man. She could empathize with everything he shared with her. Except for his wishes to settle in, both in business and personal relationships, most of what he said for prayer requests and praise items didn't center around himself but around others.

"Want to pray now?" he asked.

All she could do was nod. Something was happening here, and she wasn't sure she could deal with it.

Molly folded her hands in her lap and closed her eyes, but they shot open at the touch of Ken's larger hand on top of both of hers. His eyes were closed, and at the same time as he gave her hands a gentle squeeze, he smiled slightly and sighed. His expression was relaxed and open, like he was preparing himself to talk to an old friend.

Quickly, Molly closed her eyes again. Even though they were sharing a prayer time, she felt like she'd just invaded a private moment, studying him when he didn't know she was watching.

"Dear Lord, thank You for this time together. . . ."

She listened as he prayed for all the things they'd talked about. She'd never thought about praying out loud. When she had accepted Jesus into her heart only two short weeks ago, Robbie had done all the praying, and all she'd done was nod because she was so choked up she couldn't speak. And this time, as she listened to Ken and agreed with everything he said, she did the same, nodding at times to signal her thoughts even though no one could see her. But God could, and that was to whom they were talking.

"Amen."

Molly nodded. "Amen," she added quietly.

For a few moments, neither of them spoke. They simply sat staring, half smiling, into each other's eyes. He had nice eyes. She'd noticed his eyes the first time they met. She hadn't seen many people with such blue eyes with black hair. It set him apart. Ken Quinlan was a good-looking man.

Molly yanked her hands away. He was also her boss.

He took her withdrawal in stride. One scrap of paper at a time, they paged through her Bible and removed all her markers and read her notes, and he explained everything in an easy to understand manner.

The evening passed quickly, as it had the last time he'd

visited. As soon as they noticed how late it was, Ken apologized and headed to the door.

Molly clasped her hands in front of her. This night was truly special in ways that she couldn't begin to list. Not that she did a lot of talking, but praying with Ken in this special way, out loud and touching, gave her prayers a special emphasis, and created a bond with Ken like she'd never experienced with anyone. "Thank you for doing this with me. I'll never forget this night. Is there anything I can do to show you how much I appreciate this?"

Ken smiled, and he grasped her hands. "Yes, there is. Something unexpected came up for Saturday, so I can't do the tourist thing with you. But I'd love it if you came to church with me on Sunday."

ঌ

Molly allowed Ken to lead her from his church's foyer toward the sanctuary, where they stood in the entranceway while she got her bearings.

It was a grand old stone building, with a high vaulted ceiling and stained glass windows and carved images of Jesus in the stations of the cross adorning the walls, adding a touch of history to the grandeur. Rows and rows of wooden pews filled the large room. In the corner, an elderly lady played a massive pipe organ, the old style very much in keeping with the rest of the surroundings.

The somber organ music echoed softly, and the murmur of low voices periodically could be heard as people shuffled into their seats. Molly thought she'd seen something like it in an old magazine depicting some of the classic old churches in Europe. The Old World majesty and beauty of the place nearly took her breath away. She could feel God's presence in this magnificent place.

All the people she saw milling about radiated money. Most were older, many old enough to be her parents. This morning the only reason she'd chosen this particular outfit was because she knew Ken would be wearing a suit. Every man in the congregation wore a traditional suit and tie, and every woman was dressed in the same style. She had made the right choice. She wasn't overdressed at all.

Ken gently touched the small of her back as they ventured into the sanctuary. He spoke to her softly. "I don't know anyone here yet. I was introduced to some of the people last week, but I really wasn't in any frame of mind to be sociable."

Molly forced herself to smile and nodded. She could only imagine the difference one week would have made. So far the worst injury she'd ever sustained was a sprained ankle from her first and last attempt at skiing. She couldn't imagine actually breaking a bone. And in addition to that, she could only imagine how bumped and bruised he had been from the fall down the stairs. She wondered, if it were her, whether she would have even gone to church so soon.

Mr. Quinlan and his wife walked in, waved to them, and sat down about halfway up the aisle.

"There's Uncle Walter and Aunt Ellen. I know it's awkward for you. Don't worry. They don't expect us to sit with them. Let's sit over there."

Molly nearly fainted. Her boss was here. How could she function in the same social setting as her boss? Ever since Ken stated his request for her to accompany him, she wasn't so sure this was a good idea. Now she was positive it wasn't a good idea. All she could do was nod and follow him to a spot very close to the back row, which was fine with her.

Molly slid in first, ensuring that she sat at his right side. When they were as comfortable as possible on the hard wooden seats, she continued to study the place.

"Impressive, isn't it?"

It was past impressive, it was breathtaking. She continued to stare at the polished wooden ceiling, and the massive dangling light fixtures.

While she was still staring at the chandeliers, the lights dimmed and the volume of the organ lowered. The minister stepped forward and greeted the congregation, which Molly guessed to be about three hundred and fifty people, the place being about three- quarters filled. After a short prayer, everyone reached forward to pull their hymnals from wooden pockets in the backs of the pews in front. Everyone turned to the correct page, the volume of the organ increased, and the congregation began to sing. A few people sang in harmony, and it sounded wonderful.

Molly didn't know any of the hymns, and she didn't know how to read music, so she did her best to follow Ken, who sang beautifully. The majesty of the building and the Old World sounds of the timeless music filled Molly with a sense of awe and reverence for God's glory as they continued with a few more selections.

When they were done, the room echoed with the sounds of everyone closing the hymnals at the same time and muffled thuds of their being tucked back into the slots. Molly expected a small disturbance as the children were dismissed, as happened last week when she went to Robbie's church, but the minister started right into his sermon.

Molly tried to look around discreetly then leaned to whisper into Ken's ear. "Where are the kids?"

He leaned to whisper back. "There aren't many here. Most of the congregation is the same age as my aunt and uncle, but the kids go downstairs to children's church before the service begins."

"Oh."

The room was completely silent except for the odd shuffle as the minister began his sermon. Molly listened intently. He was speaking on faith and how faith was proved by action.

"When the waters became rough, the disciples feared the boat would sink in the storm. They saw Jesus, and Jesus was walking on the water. And they believed. But, who was the one man who had enough faith to step out onto the choppy seas?"

Molly grabbed Ken's arm. "I know the answer to that one!" she whispered to him. She didn't know if she was supposed to raise her arm, and since this wasn't a classroom, she didn't.

"Peter!" she called out.

The people in front of her flinched at the sound of her voice. Ken's arm stiffened beneath her touch. The minister stopped talking, and about half the congregation turned to stare.

Molly felt her face flame as the silence dragged.

The minister cleared his throat. "Uh, that's correct. It was indeed Peter."

At his confirmation of the correct answer, a few more people turned to stare. The minister waited for everyone's attention to return to the podium before he continued speaking.

Molly clasped her hands tightly in her lap and listened in silence. If he didn't want anyone to answer questions, why did he ask them? The man continued with his sermon, delivering a good solid message, and the congregation sat still, soaking in every word, except for one man who started to doze until his wife poked him.

They sang one more hymn at the conclusion of the service, and everyone quietly filed out of the sanctuary into the foyer, where small groups of people stood, engaged in different conversations.

"So you must be Walter's nephew. Sorry I didn't get a chance to talk to you last week. Welcome." The pastor turned to Molly. "I'm Pastor Gregory. Welcome to St. Augustine's."

"Hi. I'm Molly McNeil. I'm with him." Molly felt her face burn. She'd just referred to her new boss as "him." She wanted to leave before she did anything else incredibly stupid. Molly adjusted her purse strap on her shoulder, shuffled her Bible back and forth between her hands, then hugged it to her chest.

Pastor Gregory smiled, easing some of her nervousness. "I'm pleased to meet you, Molly. Would you and Ken like to join my wife and me, Ken's aunt and uncle, along with a few other people at our home for lunch?"

Thankfully, Ken didn't answer. He looked at her, and Molly took that to mean that he was leaving the decision up to her.

"No, not this time, but thanks for asking." She didn't want

to lie and say she was busy and hoped he wouldn't insist, because she really had no reason to turn down the invitation except for debilitating fear.

He smiled. "Well, another time, then. If you'll excuse me. . ." He glanced back and forth between herself and Ken, then left to join another group of people.

Ken's hand touched the small of her back. "Come on, let's get out of here."

She didn't need a second invitation. They were out the door without another word.

"Where would you like to go for lunch?" he asked as he fished the car keys out of his pocket.

Molly didn't know much about the church life, but she did know that it was common for the church crowd to go out for lunch following the service and that each church seemed to congregate at specific restaurants. She did want to go out for lunch, but she felt a little overwhelmed by the whole experience and didn't want to be part of a large crowd. She didn't know how Ken felt, so all she could do was hope and pray he felt the same.

She looked at his arm, knowing that his temporary handicap would be the primary factor in his choice. "I don't know. You pick."

His ears reddened. "I'm actually not all that familiar with the restaurants around here. I was hoping you could pick something, well, appropriate."

Guilt washed through her. She should have known or at least thought in advance. "I don't know this area of town. How about if you come to my place, and I'll make us something."

His face brightened. "Sure. I'd like that."

Molly chose something easy. Grilled cheese sandwiches and fries. It was also one of the few things she had enough of on hand to feed two people.

After a short prayer of thanks, Molly squeezed some catsup onto her plate, then pushed the bottle across the table.

Ken nibbled one fry without catsup and looked at her

across the table. "Well, what did you think?"

"I'm not sure. I've only been to church twice before, and it was really different."

"Every church is somewhat different. Most churches tend to be a combination of the personality of the pastor and a reflection of the lifestyle of the congregation."

"I guess that makes sense. I didn't know Mr. Quin. . .uh, your uncle, was a Christian. That's really neat."

"Most of my family are Christians."

"You're so lucky. Most of my family think I'm kinda nuts."

His eyes twinkled, and one corner of his mouth turned upwards, fighting an all-out grin. "Kinda? Can I reserve judgment?"

Molly let her mouth drop open. She'd never heard him make a flippant reply before, and she didn't know what to think.

She lowered her head and dipped a fry into the blob of catsup on her plate, then proceeded to twirl it for a while, making a design with it. "No comment."

He didn't reply but continued to grin across the table.

"So what was your church like back home?"

"Very similar."

"Tell me all about it. Where you come from, your family, how you grew up. What you do for fun."

"Fun?"

"When you're not working, what do you do?"

He smiled. "I like to cycle."

Molly tried not to stare. She couldn't imagine anything more boring. Even though she wasn't into physically challenging sports, she had tried skiing, and last summer she had made a few camping trips with her friends. "Cycle? You mean, like, on a bicycle?"

"That's usually what cycling is, Molly. Riding a bicycle."

She tried to imagine him on a bicycle. From what she'd seen so far, she doubted it was an ordinary bike like hers. And rather than her usual fare of cutoffs and a T-shirt, his clothing probably matched the bike.

"I'll bet you wear those special shorts with the padded seat, don't you?"

His ears turned red. "Of course."

"I hear the area around Winnipeg is really flat. You're going to be in for a big surprise when you try to cycle here in Vancouver, where it's really hilly."

He smiled. "Oh, I'm used to the hills. My last trip, I went to Idaho."

Molly choked on her milk. "You took your bike to Idaho?"

"Yes. That's where we decided to go this past summer."

"We?"

"A group of college friends. Before I left, we talked about meeting halfway on the Trans Canada Highway next summer, then heading south, probably from Calgary. You don't happen to cycle, do you?"

She hadn't been farther than the city limits on her bike, never mind hundreds of miles. She couldn't imagine it. "And where do you sleep?"

"We camp along the way."

Molly could see she'd greatly underestimated him. The first time she'd met him, she noticed how fit he was, and now she knew why.

He told her about a few of his long cycling trips and some of the things that happened along the way, both funny and frightening, earning him a great measure of respect in her eyes. The contrast between "Ken the Professional" and "Ken the Adventurer" astonished her and combined into a fascinating package. She'd never underestimate him again.

Time disappeared, and they only realized it was suppertime when Molly's stomach grumbled. Rather than stop in the middle of sharing their stories, they ordered pizza as they continued talking, and before they knew it, it was nearly midnight.

Molly escorted him to the door. Even though Ken still appeared comfortable after being in his suit all day, Molly was sagging. Her skirt hung limp, her blouse was hopelessly wrinkled, and her hair had fallen out of the clip long ago. She couldn't remember the last time she'd sat and talked for so long with one person. Maybe she never had. And she'd thoroughly enjoyed every minute.

She opened the door and stood in the doorway.

"Thanks for today, Ken. I know it sounds weak, but I don't know what else to say. I had a really nice time. And I really enjoyed going to your church."

He smiled. "That's great. Next Sunday, we can go to your church."

"Uh, I guess so."

He stepped closer, his eyes darkened and his expression softened. He lifted his hand, gently brushing the backs of his fingers to her cheek, then rested two fingers under her chin.

Molly's heart started to pound, both fearing and anticipating what was going to happen next.

His voice came out low and gravelly. "Good night, Molly." He tipped her chin up and tilted his head. As his head lowered, his eyes drifted shut.

Molly couldn't stop herself. As much as she knew it was a bad idea, she wanted him to kiss her.

And he did. His kiss was soft and gentle and chaste, and much too short.

Briefly, when they separated, he held her chin between his thumb and forefinger, then released her as he backed up a step.

He turned, and without saying another word, he walked away.

seven

"Kenneth? Is that you?"

"Yes, Aunt Ellen, it's me. Sorry to wake you."

They'd left the lights on, and he had been as quiet as possible when he came in, leaving him to suspect that his aunt was waiting up for him.

"It's okay; I wasn't sleeping." Ken's eyebrows raised at the sight of his aunt, already walking down the stairway, bundled in her housecoat and wearing her big fuzzy slippers. "You're certainly out late. I was beginning to worry."

"Sorry. We lost track of the time." Ken tried to keep a straight face. He'd never lost track of time like he had today. And he usually didn't do so much talking about himself, but Molly, full of innocent questions, kept pumping him for more. He didn't know who had been more embarrassed when Molly's stomach grumbled the need for supper: her, because of the surprise, or him, because he should have kept track of the time and been more courteous.

After they'd eaten, they hadn't felt the march of time until he had to fight back a yawn.

"I saw you at church with the receptionist. It was nice to see you bring her to church, especially after what happened."

Now Ken really had to struggle not to smile. He could feel Aunt Ellen's unasked hints for more information hanging above his head. He simply nodded.

"She looked so ill at ease. And you two left so quickly. One minute you were there; the next minute you were gone."

"That was only the third church service she's been to in her life. She's a new believer, and it's all quite new to her."

Aunt Ellen raised one eyebrow. He could almost imagine a neon question mark hovering above her head. "I was worried

63

that you'd had an accident or something."

He couldn't help it. Ken laughed. "Why don't you just ask me if I spent the day with Molly and what we did?"

She had the grace to blush, but said nothing.

Ken grinned, then winked at his aunt. "We had a nice day together, and that's all I'm telling. Good night, Aunt Ellen."

He climbed the stairs and went to bed, but he didn't fall asleep. All he could do was stare at the ceiling. Over and over, he went over his day with Molly. Normally she dressed casually for work, but he imagined she'd worn her best outfit to church. She may have looked prim and proper first thing in the morning, but by the time the day was over, she'd been charmingly crinkled and her hair delightfully mussed. And she'd enchanted him even more.

But, his aunt's words had been a poignant reminder. Molly was the receptionist, an employee. So far, it hadn't been important, but today, things had changed. He knew it hadn't been wise, but he'd kissed her, and she hadn't exactly pushed him away.

He couldn't help but like her. He'd only meant to disciple and help her on the way to becoming well-grounded in her faith, but they'd become distracted and talked about so many things he couldn't begin to recall them all. He'd had a wonderful time, and it seemed only natural to kiss her. Then when she responded, it was all he could do to back away.

Ken shifted positions, trying to get used to the weight of the cast resting on his stomach. He'd been having trouble sleeping and suspected that tonight would be worse, but for different reasons.

He closed his eyes, but it didn't help. Still, he could see visions of Molly.

At church, the second she'd seen his aunt and uncle, she'd changed from being in awe over the magnificent surroundings to an awkwardness he couldn't immediately put his finger on. At first he'd thought it was because of the employer/employee issue, but when she said that she didn't know his uncle was a

Christian, he was absolutely floored.

Alone in the quiet darkness, it gave him time to reflect on why this bothered him so much.

All his life, he'd been raised that it was God's will to spread the gospel and that a Christian was to let his light shine before men. Uncle Walter was not shining if Molly couldn't tell that the man she worked with for five years was a Christian. He knew Molly thought Uncle Walter was an honest man, honorable, and fair in his dealings, but plenty of non-Christians were good men. If there was nothing to set his uncle apart as a Christian, then he wasn't doing what God wanted.

In a lot of ways, he was very much like his uncle, which made him take a good hard look at his own Christian walk, and he didn't like what he saw.

By witnessing to Janice, who was clearly an unbeliever, Molly had already once reminded him that he didn't go out of his way to talk to people about Jesus. Those Ken talked to were either already believers, usually in a Bible study setting, or, if not, they were close to making a decision from someone else's evangelistic outreach and the prodding and discipling had not been instituted by him.

Would people he saw every day be able to set him apart as a Christian? Would they recognize his faith by his words and actions? If he honestly had to think about it, the answer was probably not.

Molly, on the other hand, while she didn't deliberately show off that she was a Christian, made no effort to hide it. From the first day he met her, when she awkwardly but obviously started to pause to say grace before their first meal together, he could tell beyond a shadow of a doubt where her heart was, and that was with Jesus.

Ken wanted the same. He didn't want to be simply a nice guy. He wanted not only for the world to know he was a Christian, but he wanted to be able to share his faith. There was no better place to do so than to walk side by side with a new believer. And as a new believer, he planned to be there for Molly when she had questions and to challenge her when she needed it. And likewise, she would no doubt be a challenge to him.

He smiled to himself, lying on his back in the dark, empty room. The decision brought a spark of joy to his heart. That was what he was going to do.

His uncle's church was a fine old congregation. From what he'd seen, most were well settled in their faith and continuing to grow in their own way, but it was perfectly obvious that Molly wasn't comfortable there.

He closed his eyes and smiled again. God was guiding his steps already, before he'd even consciously made his decision. Next week, he was going to be in a church setting with people more his age, and if Molly's enthusiasm and expectations for the normal order of a church service were any indication, he was going to the perfect place.

Next week, it was already confirmed. He was going to Molly's church.

❧

Molly pulled into her assigned parking spot, but before she got out of her car, she rubbed her sleepy eyes then checked to make sure she hadn't smeared her makeup.

She was dog-tired, and it was Ken's fault.

He'd left in plenty of time for her to catch a good night's sleep, but she'd spent half the night staring up at the ceiling.

Up till now, she had to admit that she had been fooling herself. He'd made his intentions perfectly clear by kissing her, and she'd been stupid enough to kiss him back. Whatever was happening, it wasn't going to work, and she had to stop it before it went any further. The man wasn't exactly her boss, but at some point, he might be. So far no one knew what the long-range plans were, but Ken wasn't there to be regular office staff. When plans were announced, they were going to be big.

Above all, she couldn't forget what happened to her best

friend. Robbie had started dating her boss's son, who had claimed to be a Christian then gradually started missing services until they'd barely attended any more. After they got engaged, he'd started an affair, and Molly was positive it hadn't been the first and told her friend so. In the end, when Robbie found out, instead of begging for forgiveness and trying to make it up to her, her ex-fiancé had Robbie fired. Robbie lost her fiancé and the job she'd held for five years within the space of an hour. Not that Mike had been a loss, but Robbie's job was.

Molly had now just passed her fifth anniversary with Quinlan Enterprises, and she had no intention of letting the same thing happen to her. Not that Ken could possibly fake being a Christian, but Robbie's experience only emphasized the fact that it was bad news for anyone to date their boss, especially since he came from a moneyed background, and Molly grew up in a rather seedy neighborhood, something she hoped he would never find out. She couldn't allow herself to be weak, no matter how nice he was or how much she liked him. It was too dangerous, both personally and professionally.

As she entered the building, a strange emotion gripped her when she walked past the reception area and past her desk. Correction, her old desk. As much as she desired a promotion, she missed her duties as receptionist. She liked meeting people and talking on the phone. It gave her a great deal of satisfaction to know that as soon as Ken's arm healed, he would no longer be needing her as his assistant and she could return to her regular duties.

She hustled into the lunchroom to get her first cup of coffee for the day, but instead of hanging around to chat, she immediately went to her desk.

Ken and Mr. Quinlan arrived a few minutes later. Mr. Quinlan merely nodded at her on his way past, as he did every morning when he walked by her at her usual station in the reception area. Ken, on the other hand, smiled and slowed his pace, just to make sure she acknowledged him with a returning smile.

Instead of going to his desk beside her, Ken continued on to talk to the office manager and shut the door. Molly worked by herself for nearly an hour until Ken returned.

"Molly, can you please come into the boardroom with me?"

Molly cringed. Her first thought was that she was in trouble over something she might have done wrong. After all, the things she had been given were far from the usual duties given to a receptionist. She'd taken a few business courses at night school, but she didn't have any actual practical experience. She was just getting that now—the hard way.

Was he going to tell her she was doing a poor job, and her services were no longer required? Her next thought was even more frightening. After he'd kissed her last night, was he planning on getting her in a private room, where no one would interrupt, and kiss her again? Part of her was terrified he would, yet part of her wanted exactly that.

Molly mentally kicked herself. What was she thinking? The man was a professional—who held the power to have her fired.

She followed him into the boardroom in silence. When he closed the door behind them, her heartbeat quickened.

"I thought we'd best do this in private."

Molly's knees started trembling. Her feet remained glued to the floor, and she wached as Ken walked to the computer, pulled out the chair in front of it, then dragged another chair beside the one he'd already moved, and sat in that one.

When she didn't move, he turned to look at her, eyebrows raised. "I need this done right away, and I can't take the chance that it will be overheard while I dictate it. We don't have much time."

She heaved a sigh of relief and her knees weakened as she forced her feet to move and lowered herself into the chair. He dictated a disciplinary letter concerning one of the production supervisors while she typed, quickly proofread it, then hit the print button.

Ken checked his watch. "I have a lunch meeting to go to, but this one I don't need you to take notes. I'll be seeing Joseph about the letter as soon as I get back. Make sure you're free at two-thirty, because after that I'll have to go over the quarterly totals for the branch offices and approve them before I can leave."

All Molly could do was nod and try not to feel slighted that their meeting was all business after all.

"Thanks, Molly. I've got to run. See you later."

Ken dashed out the door, leaving Molly alone in the large and empty boardroom.

Molly returned to her desk, absently adding some totals. She'd prayed for their relationship at work to be strictly professional. From Ken's behavior in the boardroom, she'd been given what she prayed for. Why did she not like it?

ᵒᵃ

Molly raced in the door after the Bible study at Robbie's house just in time to catch the phone before the answering machine clicked on. Strangely, it was no surprise to hear Ken's voice.

"Oh, good, you're home. How did it go?"

Molly smiled ear to ear as she shuffled out of her jacket and tossed her Bible and purse into the table. "It was great! Too bad you couldn't come. And it went just like you said it would, with the way everyone prayed with prayer requests and praise items, and someone really did write everything down in a prayer journal, and we talked about all sorts of things, and I got to meet some more people from my new church, and we had cake and coffee afterwards, and well, it was great."

She paused to breathe, kicking herself for running off at the mouth after Ken's simple question.

After a short pause where neither of them spoke, Ken's voice came out low and husky. "Did you miss me?"

"Yes, I. . ." She cut herself off. She had missed him. Of course a lot of her prayer concerns had to do with him, and since the Bible study was at her best friend's house, it was easy to share. Molly cleared her throat. "Yes, it was too bad you had to work late. Robbie's husband also became a Christian at a young age; you would have enjoyed talking to him, and there were a few people there who became Christians as adults, so it was good for me to talk to them."

She could hear the smile in his voice. "I see."

For once, she didn't comment.

"Another reason I'm calling is that Uncle Walter is going out of town tomorrow, and I have to take his place at a Chamber of Commerce function tomorrow night. I was wondering if you'd like to come with me. I'll need help keeping track of who's who since I've never met any of these people before, except for Trevor Chapman."

She didn't know whether to be relieved that he was calling about business or not. She also didn't want to know why it would matter. "Sure, I can go. I guess I can take some kind of notes."

He laughed. "It's true that it's a business function, but I don't want anyone to think you're my secretary, Molly. What I need is for everyone to think you're my date."

eight

Molly lifted one arm to carefully snip the price tag off her new dress, stood on her tiptoes, and tried to get the best view she could using the bathroom mirror. She'd never attended a Chamber dinner before. She'd never attended any kind of business function. Receptionists didn't exactly get engraved invitations to those kind of events. Therefore, she had no idea what to do, what to say, and especially no idea what to wear. Ken had given her a few guidelines, and with his suggestions in mind, Molly had done her best to choose something suitable on her way home from work.

The lady at the store had helped a lot. When Molly told her what she needed the dress for, the woman told her she had the perfect selection, especially considering her hair, and ran to get it before Molly could say anything further.

As she turned around and tried to get a rear view, she still wasn't sure it was right, but she hadn't had enough time to make a proper choice. She'd never bought a dress in one evening, unless it was an impulse item and on sale. Even then, it was an all-day excursion because she would end up making at least six trips back to the store before she actually bought the item that caught her eye.

She picked the price tag out of the sink where it had fallen and shuddered. If she had impulses like this too often, it would bankrupt her.

However, she didn't have to worry about things like this ever again. Tonight was going to be the first and last time. She tried to figure out who she knew that was still single, because the next time she wore this expensive dress would be to someone's wedding.

The buzzer for the entrance sounded, making Molly's heart

pound. It was Ken. He was early. She ran to push the button to let him in the main entrance and hoped he had to wait a long time for the elevator. She had meant to put her hair up for a touch of class, something she seldom did, even though she knew the unruly mass would never stay that way. Truly, she had at least started out with the best of intentions. Molly abandoned all her grand plans, dashed back into the bathroom to hastily apply her lipstick, two swipes of eye shadow, and a couple flicks of mascara before she heard the sharp knock on her door.

❧

Molly opened the door wide. "Is this okay?" She twirled around in the open doorway.

She stopped suddenly and faced him, her arms slightly spread, making direct eye contact, not giving him time to cover his initial reaction.

Ken opened his mouth, then snapped it shut. She'd looked very nice and presentable on Sunday, but today, she looked. . . different. The cream-colored dress she wore was perfect for the occasion, a combination of silky fabric with a bit of lace to make it extremely feminine yet still suitable for a business function, but it had an undertone of what he could only call sass. A little voice in the back of his mind reminded him that she had purchased this dashing little number just for him, for tonight. While it showed nothing indecent, she looked ravishing. She was every man's dream come true—a gorgeous and classy woman, wanting to look her best just for him, yet still maintaining her innocence, and for the evening, she was his.

All he could do was stare. This was Molly.

"You don't like it," she mumbled and looked down to the floor.

"Oh, but I do!" he exclaimed. Ken cleared his throat and lowered both the pitch and volume of his voice, trying to recapture a bit of dignity. "I mean, I do like it. You look. . ." Words failed him. He wanted to show her how much he liked it. He wanted to touch her, to hold her, to run his hands down the smooth fabric. He wanted to kiss her, and not to stop like he had on Sunday. He wanted to kiss her well and good.

He tried not to blush. He promised himself he was going to stick to business and to be firm in his resolve. The only time he would allow himself to see her outside the office or functions concerning work was to be for church-related activities. That meant Wednesday night Bible study and Sunday services. And maybe a nice long lunch after church.

Ken cleared his throat and smiled politely. "You look nice."

Her unsure little smile made him stand straighter.

"I just have to go comb my hair and I'll be ready to go. Please come in."

Rather than be snoopy, when Molly disappeared into the bathroom Ken closed the apartment door behind him but remained there. A pretty pair of shoes the same color as her dress sat on a small rubber mat. They were sleek and sassy, and had killer heels.

"Okay, let's go." She leaned her hand against the wall and slipped a foot into one of the ridiculous shoes.

"You're not really going to wear those, are you?"

She wiggled her foot until it was all the way in, then bent over and picked up the other shoe, leaned back against the wall for balance, and slid the shoe on her other foot. "I'm not even going to answer that."

"How are you going to walk?"

As she straightened, a taller than usual Molly stood in front of him. She snorted in a way Ken thought quite unfeminine, greatly contrasting with the intriguing combination of the dress and high shoes along with a matching purse that he hadn't seen before. In direct defiance of his question, she stalked past him, stood outside the door, and jingled her keys in the air.

Ken couldn't help himself. He laughed. He was still laughing as he walked into the hallway and waited for her to lock up. "Sorry," he said, knowing that by laughing he was showing her he really wasn't, "but far be it from me to understand women's shoes."

"You're just jealous because your shoes are boring."

He'd never considered shoes to have a personality. They kept his feet warm and dry. He thought the smartest thing to do would be to not reply.

"And do you know for sure where we're going?"

Ken nodded. "It's close to the Stevens Building."

"Yes, but do you know *exactly* where it is?"

"I have the address."

Molly snorted again. This time Ken didn't laugh.

"I thought so. I'll give you directions."

⌘

The Chamber of Commerce dinner was a surprisingly pleasant affair.

Molly dutifully stood beside Ken whenever he spoke to someone else he hadn't met before and tried not to laugh every time he not-so-discreetly glanced down to her shoes. Her feet were killing her, but she would die before she told him so.

All of the married business owners or executives had their wives or husbands with them, and the few single men present had brought dates. Molly could tell the difference. The wives held their own in conversations, the girlfriends tended to cling. Molly refused to cling and did her best to contribute what she could to the conversations, telling herself that it was just as easy talking to these prominent business owners and managers as it was over the phone, rather than leaving them indefinitely on hold, which she considered rude.

She knew who many of these people were, having spoken to them before. She didn't tell anyone she was only the receptionist, but Ken introduced her anyway.

Tonight she tried her best not to run off at the mouth or get distracted. She was here to help Ken schmooze with those who were to be his peers. Amongst all these important people, all dressed in their fine clothes, it was easy to remember to act dignified and, mostly, to be quiet.

Ken often asked if she knew who some of the people were,

and for the most part, Molly could tell once she heard them speak. She made it into a game to match the voices she'd spoken to so often on the phone with the faces.

After allowing a respectable amount of making the rounds, the emcee requested that everyone please be seated for dinner. Cards at the place settings indicated they were to sit at the same table as Trevor Chapman and his wife and a couple that Molly had never spoken to before.

She could hardly wait to sit down and rest her aching feet, but Ken's touch stopped her. "I just wanted to give you a word of advice, Molly," he whispered in her ear. "They won't be saying grace here, and I generally find it more comfortable to just quietly close my eyes in private for a quick word of thanks, with my hands folded in my lap under the table. It would be different if it were just the two of us, but this is quite a crowd, and it's a business function. I've found out the hard way that if you're too obvious, it makes people ill at ease, and a chance to speak about it later is lost."

His words immediately recalled the first time they'd dined together, and neither knew the other was a Christian. While she wondered if anyone here was as well, she took his words to heart. For herself, she didn't care. The people at the office acted a little strange at first, but they quickly got used to her praying over her lunch bag. Only one person had made a snide comment, but she'd told him what she thought of his rude remark, although afterward she was sorry she'd snapped at him. She couldn't afford to do that here, but like Ken, she also wouldn't ignore God just because she was out in public.

The meal was served, and conversation flowed at their table.

Heather Chapman tapped Molly on the shoulder, as they sat side by side. "Molly, I just had to tell you this. I thought you'd like to know that Trevor bought that allergy product you suggested, and we asked for Missykins to be freshly bathed before we arrived, and the symptoms have been reduced to a minimum. It means so much to our granddaughter to have

Grampa play with her little dog. I wish I could find a way to thank you."

"Maybe Trevor could sign a one-year contr—" A nudge at her ankle cut off her words.

Ken quelled her with one glance, then turned to the Chapmans. "That's so good to hear. I had a dog when I was a boy, and I have nothing but fond memories of all the family playing with him."

Molly clamped her lips shut. She was only teasing. Couldn't the man understand a joke?

Heather Chapman pulled out a small pocket-sized photo album entitled *Gramma's Brag Book* and proceeded to show off a score of photographs of their granddaughter, a few of which featured Missykins.

Molly couldn't help but smile. One day she would learn the little girl's name.

Immediately following the dinner, the mayor was called to the front, and between the dull monotone of his voice, the aftereffects of the delicious meal, and the relief to be off her aching feet, Molly struggled to keep her eyes open. Her eyes had almost drifted shut when a gentle touch on her hand in her lap startled her to complete wakefulness. Ken's fingers slowly intertwined with hers and remained linked.

Instead of staring at their joined hands, she looked up to his face. He smiled warmly.

"I agree," he whispered. "It can't be much longer. You can do it."

Heat rose in her face. She'd been caught almost dozing off. Abruptly, she turned to stare intently at the podium, knowing that as long as she could feel Ken's gentle grip, she would remain fully alert.

The mayor's words droned on in oblivion while Molly tried to figure out first why Ken was holding her hand and, second, what she should do about it.

The first and most common reason for holding hands like this was mutual affection. She couldn't deny that she liked him. The memory of his short but very poignant kiss still lingered in the forefront of her memory, which only emphasized that she had allowed things to go too far. For now, she would enjoy it for the brief time it lasted, but tonight, she would have to tell him they couldn't allow things to continue. She repeated over and over in her mind that Ken was her supervisor.

Trying to rationalize it as best she could and trying not to enjoy the warmth of his hand too much, she convinced herself that if she pulled her hand away she would embarrass him. Everyone was supposed to think she was there as his date.

Maybe her fears were for nothing. Maybe the reason he was holding her hand was because of that very reason. A few of the married couples were also holding hands, but she suspected it was for the same reason, to keep each other awake.

The thought lifted a weight off her shoulders. It was as simple as that. He'd made it clear this was a business function, and at the end of the evening, before he left for the night, she would simply have a short talk with him, just to make sure that that was the case.

For the moment, she would simply enjoy the comfort of her hand within his, and she would enjoy it without guilt because she knew the reasons.

❧

The speech dragged on another fifteen minutes after he had taken her hand in his, and Ken smiled to himself. His desperate plan continued to work. Not only was Molly staying fully awake throughout what was surely the most boring speech he'd ever heard in his life, but the feel of her hand in his kept him awake, too. A few discreet glances around the room confirmed his suspicions that they were not the only ones so affected. Unfortunately, the mayor was the only one not to notice his effect on the crowd.

Ken glanced down for a moment at Molly's small hand clasped in his. She'd been good enough to attend the function with him, and he hated the thought of her being so bored she was falling asleep. Short of nudging her, which wouldn't have been very delicate or discreet, he didn't know what to do. He could tell that she had been struggling to stay awake and was losing the battle. Now, if he noticed her starting to drift, he could give her hand a gentle squeeze and no one would be the wiser. He could well imagine how embarrassed she would be at being caught nodding off.

He could also admit to himself that it was a good excuse to touch her. And this was another reminder that he couldn't allow this to continue. Even though it was hard to do in their present setting, he again had to remind himself that Molly was an employee. He had no business crossing the line, which, by holding her hand, he was doing again.

He continued to ignore the droning speech. For now, he might manage to fool himself that he was holding hands purely to keep them both awake. However, at the end of the evening, their relationship would be back to purely business and church-related functions.

At the close of the speech, Molly quickly withdrew her fingers and was the first to applaud.

Coffee and wine flowed as the crowd mingled once again, signaling his cue to leave. They said their good-byes and were soon back in his uncle's car. The entire drive, Molly chattered incessantly. Ken listened politely, nodding on cue, hoping she couldn't see him trying to fight a grin. He was actually getting used to it, and he liked the musical quality of her voice. As he looked for an empty space in the visitor park-ing at Molly's apartment complex, he smiled at yet another amusing anecdote.

ð

Knowing he was only being a gentleman, Molly smiled politely and had allowed him to escort her all the way to her apartment. Molly knew she had chattered incessantly but couldn't help it. Every time she felt a lull in the conversation, she found herself filling it. She knew she was only doing it because she was nervous, but even knowing so, she still couldn't stop. By the time he pulled into a parking spot, she was sure he would be only too happy to be rid of her, but to her surprise, he had turned off the engine and exited the car.

Her fingers shook as she dug the keys out of her purse, then continued to shake as she inserted the key in the lock, making them tinkle. She stepped inside and toed off her shoes, vowing never to wear them again, then turned to thank him for the evening, but he followed her inside and closed the door.

Molly blinked. "Uh, would you like a cup of coffee or some tea, maybe?"

"No, I just wanted to thank you for the evening in a more private setting than the community hallway."

Molly gulped. The only way she could think of for a man to say a private good-bye was to kiss a woman good night. She had already told herself that it would be a bad idea. She waited on pins and needles, except he wasn't making any attempt to step closer.

"I also wanted to tell you how much I've come to value you in the short time we've known each other. You're a tremendous asset to the company in the way you greet people when they come inside for the first time, in addition to the way you handle everyone on the phone."

She knotted her brows. *Company? Asset?*

"You've also been a tremendous help to me both at the office and now tonight. I wanted to say thank you properly."

A million thoughts zinged through her head as she tried to figure out what he meant by "properly." As different as the evening was from a typical date, she had enjoyed herself, except for the mayor's boring speech, but the meal was lovely. The dessert was absolutely heavenly. If his idea of a proper thank-you was to offer to pay for the dress, she just might scream.

Her heart pounded as he stepped closer, but instead of bending to kiss her, he reached out his unencumbered hand and grasped one of her hands. Butterflies fluttered in her stomach as he ran his thumb up and down her wrist.

"I also wanted to say that I appreciate everything you've

done for me. I look forward to working with you as my assistant. I believe tonight will be the only time we'll need to see each other outside of the office for a business function, so I won't be interrupting your social calendar again."

At his smile, her heart constricted. Interrupting her social calendar? She didn't have a social calendar. If he was saying what she thought he was saying, it was that he didn't want to have anything to do with her except for work. While it was exactly what she had convinced herself she wanted to hear, it bothered her to hear him say it.

"Of course, that doesn't include this Wednesday night's Bible study. I look forward to that very much. I enjoy answering your questions and hope I can be of continuing help to you as you continue to grow in your Christian walk. And I look forward to attending a study with people my age." He grinned, making her heart beat faster. "You've got to admit, the average age of my uncle's congregation is at least a decade and a half beyond me."

Molly gulped. He'd been a great help to her so far, and she had invited him to attend a Bible study at Robbie's house since he didn't know anyone in town yet except for business acquaintances and his family. Ken had a wealth of knowledge accumulated since childhood, and she was eager to learn all he had to teach her. She experienced an unexpected relief to know he was still planning on doing that with her.

He leaned down, and Molly closed her eyes to feel the softness of his lips as he brushed a soft kiss against her cheek, then stood upright once more.

"If there's ever anything I can do for you, you be sure and let me know."

All she could do was stare up at him.

"And I'll see you Sunday morning. Thanks for inviting me."

Her heart pounded. She seemed to recall that he had invited himself, but her mind was reeling too fast to contradict him.

He gave her hand one last gentle squeeze and released her. "Good night, Molly."

The door closed behind him, and she heard his muffled footsteps fade down the hall.

≈

Ken smiled as he left the elevator and headed back to the car. He had clearly outlined his position, and she had readily agreed. He hadn't wanted to separate business from pleasure, but he had no other alternative. To do otherwise wouldn't be proper.

From now on, the only personal interaction they would have would be for the purposes of evangelistic outreach, which was helping a new believer become grounded.

It wasn't exactly what he wanted, but there was no other way. Outside of work, he would only see Molly for Bible studies and church services.

And he'd never looked forward to Sunday so much.

nine

Ken pushed the button for Molly's apartment, then started for her apartment when she buzzed the lock open. She was waiting for him when he arrived at her door.

"You're wearing a tie."

"Yes, I. . ." Ken raised his hand to pat the object in question. Today Molly was wearing a casual outfit that he'd seen her wear to work.

"You've got to take it off."

"We're going to church, Molly. I haven't gone to church without a tie since I was a boy. As it is, I should be wearing the jacket."

Before he could protest, Molly reached forward and tugged the tie into a wide circle around his neck. He didn't want to fight her, especially when she seemed so determined, so he let her remove it. Unfortunately, rather than simply opening it and slipping it over his head, she pulled it apart before he could protest. He was getting sick of asking Uncle Walter to tie all his ties for him. Finally he'd gotten to the point where he had enough strength without pain in his fingers to squeeze a bit of his hairgel into his right hand and make a decent job at fixing his hair by himself. If nothing else, he was experiencing a lesson in humility like never before.

Ken cringed as she threw the tie inside, hoping it had at least landed on the table. "Let's go," she said and physically turned him around, pushing him out the door before he could make an attempt to retrieve it.

They pulled into a parking lot bustling with cars and people. A few young boys were playing catch in an empty portion of the lot then stopped when a woman called to them from somewhere Ken couldn't identify. He was surprised to think the woman would allow the children to play outside before church, taking the chance they would mess their clothes. As the boys ran past, he noted they were wearing jeans and sneakers.

On their way past, one of the boys dropped their softball. Ken picked it up, then wondered how he was going to throw it with his right hand and not take the chance of sending it terribly awry and hitting a car in the rapidly filling parking lot.

"You're not going to throw it, are you?" Molly asked, confirming that she also doubted his ability.

He tossed it in the air a couple of inches and caught it just fine, but he decided not to take the chance and throw it.

"Do you have a baseball mitt for your right hand? I can catch with my left hand, but I can only throw with my right." Molly covered her mouth with her hands as she looked down at his left hand and the cast. "You can catch, but you can't throw. So literally, that's what you'd be doing. Playing catch. Just catch. Get it?" She laughed behind her hands.

Ken didn't think she was being very funny. He handed her the softball. "Here, smarty. I can take a hint. You throw it."

They were both saved from taking the chance of throwing it off the mark. One of the boys ran back to them, Molly handed him the ball, and he ran to rejoin his friends.

A man in a suit, tie included, stood with a well-dressed woman at the main entrance, handing out bulletins and greeting people as they entered.

Ken nudged Molly and leaned slightly to talk quietly in her ear. "See. He's wearing a suit and tie."

Molly snorted. "Yeah. And he's nearly the only one who is. I've only been here a couple of times before, but I did notice that."

She smiled as she accepted the bulletin, and they entered.

People were everywhere, chatting and laughing. Not a single man of those he could see in the congregation wore a suit or a tie. Many people wore jeans, both men and women. He'd never seen anything like it. Music echoed from what he assumed was the sanctuary, only it wasn't an organ, it sounded like a whole band, and he thought he recognized the song from one of his CDs.

As they continued to walk toward the sanctuary, he saw a young couple about their age standing in the middle of a small group of people. The woman held a toddler in her arms, and the man was showing pictures to everyone surrounding him. From the oohs and aahs of the people around, he wondered if they were showing off baby pictures, although the child in her arms, while cute, was not a baby anymore.

Like a typical woman, Molly gazed at the group with stars in her eyes. He thought Molly would make a wonderful mother and wondered if he would be a good father someday. He'd come from a happy home, his parents were still happily married, and they had been good role models. In the back of his mind, he wondered what kind of wife Molly would be for whatever man could keep up with her.

"That's Edwin and Doreen. They go to Robbie's Bible study. Come on. I want to see their pictures. On Wednesday night he said he'd be bringing them today."

Ken smiled. He'd never wanted to see baby pictures before, even when he knew the parents, but today, the idea appealed to him.

Molly grabbed his hand and pulled. He liked the unstated familiarity the gesture implied.

Together they peeked over a few shoulders at the pictures while the man flipped through the pile.

"And here's Baby B, my pride and joy," Edwin said.

Ken whispered into Molly's ear. "Those are dogs!"

"Aren't they cute? One day I want to get a puppy!"

Ken's mind reeled as he watched the man slowly flip through more puppy pictures. On one hand, he could well imagine life in suburbia, coming home to a wife, a few kids, and a barking dog. On the other hand, the way this couple was fawning over their dog pictures, he thought they were a little strange.

"Hi, Molly," a deep voice resounded from behind him.

Ken turned to where a tall man stood directly behind him. A short little woman gave Molly a big hug.

"Ken, this is Robbie, my best friend, and this is her husband, Garrett." Molly beamed ear to ear. "I introduced them to each other. And Garrett's a forest ranger."

Ken blinked, unable to figure out what one had to do with the other.

Garrett glanced down to take note of the cast, then back up again, and shook his hand. "Ah, so you're Ken. We've heard so much about you. We've been praying for you." Garrett's voice lowered so only Ken could hear his next comment. "I think you're going to need it."

Ken didn't think he wanted to know the details. "Thank you," he said, averting his gaze to Molly, who wouldn't make eye contact.

Molly pulled him into the sanctuary. Instead of pews, there were rows of padded stacking chairs. Except for a single cross at the front, the room was void of any decoration. The starkness of the room led him to believe that this was more a multipurpose room than a specific sanctuary.

People milled everywhere, and the room was filled with the buzz of voices; the only difference between here and the foyer was that in the quasi-sanctuary the voices were slightly softer. A group of teens hovered in the back, laughing and cajoling each other before they shuffled to their seats, not with their parents, but with other teens, the sole occupants of the back three rows of that side.

On a slightly elevated stage, just as he had suspected, was a whole band. There was a drummer, an older gentleman who was wearing a suit but no tie playing a bass guitar, and a younger man wearing faded jeans and playing a bright red electric guitar. In profile, a very pregnant woman played the glossy black grand piano. Ken couldn't believe his eyes at the odd combination.

Not long after they sat, more people filed in to take their

seats. Ken found the place a little overwhelming, but at the same time, it had a certain appeal, despite the lack of order.

The lights dimmed, the room quieted, and a man in a matching shirt and slacks, with a tie and no suit jacket, stepped to the podium. He welcomed everyone present; a screen lowered from the ceiling; the congregation stood; and everyone sang a rousing chorus that he recognized from a CD he had in his car, complete with hands clapping to the rhythm. Ken couldn't believe it.

At the close of the song, the man, who was evidently the pastor, encouraged everyone to greet those around them. After the clamor died down, he read a few highlights from the bulletin, then called one of the teenagers from the back corner to the microphone.

The youth shuffled his feet as he nervously looked around at the congregation, then down to the floor. He tapped the microphone with one finger, blew into it, then backed up a step.

"Uh, yeah," he stammered, as he finally raised his eyes. "I wanted to tell you all about how we're doing for our raising money thing for the youth group going to Bible Quest this year. Uh, like, we're still a few hundred bucks short 'cause we need to rent a bus. Like, lots of the kids in the youth group don't come to church, you know, and their parents aren't gonna be paying anything. So we're going to have like a banquet or something next weekend after church. It's going to be lunch. Tickets are five bucks and come see me or Ryan and I'll sell you some. Someone will phone you during the week to tell you what to bring, because it's a potluck. That's all I was gonna say."

The boy shuffled back to his seat, where a couple of his friends patted him on the back for a job well-done.

Ken remembered his days of attending youth group. Most of his memories of his youth were happy, except for being called Kenny. But what stuck in his mind was the youth's comment that many of the group wanting to attend a youth-oriented Christian function came from non-Christian homes.

He wanted to do everything he could to see that no one who wanted to attend would be left out.

The pastor called the ushers to the front for the offering and led the congregation in a short prayer.

He couldn't provide transportation himself, but he could help pay for the bus. His biggest problem would be his inability to write. He leaned to whisper to Molly. "Can you pull the offering envelope out of your bulletin?"

Her raised eyebrows registered her surprise, but she scrambled to pull it out, then studied it as if she'd never seen an offering envelope before.

"Quickly, Molly. Just write *youth group* on it and leave the rest blank."

She dug a pen out of her purse, scribbled in the middle of the envelope, then froze, the pen hovering above the total line. "How much?"

Since he still couldn't write out a check or legibly sign a credit card receipt, he had to pay for everything he purchased in cash. Therefore, he had a sizable amount of money in his wallet. He hoped it was enough to pay for the bus. "I don't know exactly how much I've got on me; I don't have time to count it. Leave it blank."

Molly handed him the envelope as the basket drew closer. Ken emptied all the bills from his wallet into the envelope, licked it, and tossed it into the basket in the nick of time.

A different man stepped forward to lead everyone to worship in song. It included one hymn, played with bass guitar and drums in a way Ken had never heard and couldn't quite decide if he liked. The rest of the worship songs were contemporary choruses, none lacking in commitment or sincerity, and he found the simple words and easy-to-follow melodies moved his heart in a way he hadn't expected. Halfway through the worship time, the children were called to the front for a short prayer before they were dismissed to their classrooms, when they ran out of the room hooting and screaming. A few parents laughed and groaned in frustration from their own children's antics, and the worship time continued.

When the pastor returned to the podium for the sermon, everyone settled in with their Bibles and followed the sermon notes on the back of the bulletin. Ken peeked over Molly's shoulder, as he had not brought his own Bible, still not sure of his ability to hold it steady and turn pages with one hand. He expected that in one more week, he would have enough strength and mobility in his fingers to manage, but not yet.

Every once in awhile, the pastor paused to ask a question, and to Ken's surprise, many people called out the answer. When a key point was made, people freely called out a resounding "Amen," and once someone from the back row called out a friendly heckling joke in response to one of the pastor's questions, at which the congregation laughed.

Ken had never been to a service like this in his life.

Right on time, the pastor drew his sermon to a close, and everyone bowed their heads in prayer. At the pastor's "Amen" everyone opened their eyes. The worship team had returned to the front of the church, and the words for "Jesus Loves Me" appeared on the screen.

Ken smiled. He hadn't sung "Jesus Loves Me" for years, in fact, probably not since he was ten years old. He sang whole-heartedly with the rest of the congregation, and after the third verse, the accompaniment cut out and the congregation repeated the first verse, creating a unique resonance in the large room.

The sincerity and beauty of the unaccompanied voices' singing filled his heart like he'd never experienced. An attitude of sincere worship flowed through the building, touching his soul.

Ken closed his eyes as he sang, letting the simple words really sink in. Jesus loved everyone in that room, and singly, Jesus loved him, too. Even though he'd known it for years, something moved deep inside his heart.

When the song ended, a silence filled the room. In a soft and gentle voice, the pastor asked that if anyone wanted to ask Jesus into their hearts they should step forward, and everyone else was invited to have coffee and visit.

A few people rose and stepped forward, and many others began gathering their belongings to get a cup of coffee.

Ken turned to Molly to ask if she wanted to stay, but his voice caught. Molly's eyes were still closed, and tears streamed down her cheeks. All he could do was stare.

Her eyes drifted open, she brushed her sleeve across her eyes rather indelicately, smearing black smudges, sniffled, then smiled at him, her eyes wide and still glassy with tears. She'd never looked more beautiful.

Her voice cracked as she spoke. "Jesus loves me, Ken."

Ken couldn't breathe. At that moment, he knew that not only did Jesus love Molly, but he loved her, too.

ten

Naturally Molly didn't have a tissue in her purse, so she quickly introduced Ken to some of the people who had attended the Bible study at Robbie's house and dashed off to the ladies' room to blow her nose and do a temporary repair to her face.

When she returned, Ken was still with her friends. He joined very little in the various conversations going around the circle of people, and every time a child screamed, he flinched. His eyes darted back and forth through the crowd continuously, as if he couldn't believe what he was seeing.

She rejoined the group as one of the youths approached, asking who was going to buy tickets for their fundraiser lunch the following Sunday. Garrett and Edwin reached for their wallets, as did Ken, but as soon as his hand touched his pocket, his hand froze.

Molly knew he'd suddenly remembered he didn't have any money left on him, but she wasn't going to tell anyone that he'd already given it all to the youth group. Instead, she put her hand on his arm. "No, Ken, this is my church, so it's my treat," she said loudly enough for everyone in the group to hear. She pulled out enough money for two tickets, then realized that by buying him a ticket, she was again inviting him to attend church with her next week.

After she tucked the tickets into her wallet, she glanced over her shoulder. "Want a cookie? It looks like if we don't get one now, the kids will get them all."

His eyes widened as he turned to face the refreshment table. A little boy busily helped himself to three cookies and a few sugar cubes and then ran off to join his friends.

"Uh, no, thank you. I think I'll pass."

Garrett stepped closer to Ken. "I hear this might be a little different than what you're used to."

Again, Ken's eyes darted from side to side, this time focusing on a few people sharing some outrageously funny joke. Everyone in the small group roared with laughter, then the men smacked each other firmly on the backs while one of them reenacted a golf swing.

Ken's hand went up to where the knot of his tie should have been, his fingers grasped thin air, and he quickly dropped his hand to his side. "I have to admit I'm used to a more, uh, conservative setting."

Molly laid one hand on his arm. "Would you like a coffee? I'll pour it for you."

He shook his head. "No, thank you."

She couldn't blame him. She couldn't imagine what it must be like to be limited to using only one hand, and the wrong one at that.

"If you don't mind, I need one. I'll be right back."

Before he could protest, she hurried away. Since there were only a couple of people at the coffee machine, she wouldn't have a long wait.

From a distance, she saw Garrett and Ken talking in her absence. At something Garrett said, Ken nodded, and both men broke out into wide grins. Molly stared at the two of them. Ken was such a handsome man.

As they continued talking, Garrett broke out into a full laugh, making Molly wonder what it was that Ken said and hope it wasn't about her, even though she suspected it might be.

She hurried to pour herself only half a cup of coffee and didn't bother to take a cookie. Instead, she returned to Ken's side. "Are you guys talking about me?"

Ken's ears turned red.

Garrett gave her a cocky grin that spoke for itself. "Would we do that?"

"Never answer a question with a question," Molly mumbled. Neither of them said anything to give her a hint, and she wasn't sure she wanted to know.

Garrett cleared his throat. "Are you two coming for lunch? Everyone's going to the same place as usual."

All she could do was glance at Ken, who was being unusually quiet. Without meaning to, she looked down at his fingers sticking out of the cast. Only having been to what she knew was the local lunch hangout pancake restaurant twice, she wasn't quite sure of the menu and didn't know if they served anything a person wouldn't have to cut. While Ken would never give any indication of being ill at ease, she didn't want to put him on the spot, and she certainly didn't want to embarrass him if he had difficulty amongst strangers. As it was, he'd taken his chances at the Chamber dinner. He was lucky the menu was stir-fried steak with rice, but afterwards she remembered his comments that he was prepared to go through the drive-thru hamburger joint on the way home if he couldn't eat the dinner.

She couldn't do that to him.

"Ken and I have other plans. Maybe another time, okay?"

Robbie looked at her funny, but she wasn't about to explain herself. Not that she wanted to give her friend the impression that anything was going on between her and Ken, but she didn't have time to explain.

Ken's eyebrows raised momentarily, and he turned back to Garrett and extended his hand. Garrett grasped it and they exchanged a handshake. "It was a pleasure meeting you, Garrett, and your charming wife. I'm sure we'll see each other again soon."

Garrett nodded. "Yeah. Bible study at our house, Wednesday night. I hope you don't have to work late every Wednesday."

"No, something unusual came up last week. I'll be there. Thanks."

Molly could barely contain her excitement. Not only would Ken be a great addition to the group, but since he didn't know anyone in town, she hoped he and Garrett could get to know each other better. After learning of Ken's long bicycle trips, she was sure they would have a lot to share about various adventures in the great outdoors.

They took their leave quietly, but once in the car, Ken turned to her without starting it. "So what are these other plans we're supposed to have?"

She felt her face flush, so she winked to try to bluff away her nervousness. "The plan is to go somewhere where you don't go hungry."

"Yeah. After all, I'm a growing boy."

Molly's mouth gaped open, unable to figure out his uncharacteristic comment. "Uh, something like that."

"Well, you show me where you want to go. I just have to make a short stop first."

It didn't take a lot of guessing at what he was planning when he made a stop at the bank machine. She was going to offer to treat him, but if he was going to all this trouble to get some money, she suspected he was determined to pay. She didn't want to bruise his ego, so she said nothing. Besides, it gave her some extra time to decide on a small family restaurant she knew well.

❧

Molly's choice was, once again, a good one. Fortunately they didn't have to wait long for a table and were soon seated.

The food was excellent. After a pleasant meal and enjoyable conversation over their lunch, Molly rested her elbows on the table and cradled her coffee cup in her hands. "Well? What did you think?"

He blinked and stared at her. "The food's good here."

"Not that. I meant this morning."

Briefly he looked into his coffee cup, glanced around the restaurant, then back at her. "I like your friends."

"You'll meet most of them again on Wednesday. I think you'll really like Garrett. I've known him for years."

She smiled bright and wide and Ken smiled back. He still didn't know what to make of the service, but he didn't want to think about that. He couldn't take his eyes off of Molly. Her eyes sparkled as all her attention focused on him. If she kept looking at him like that, he didn't know how he could carry on a conversation. "Garrett seems nice, and he's quite fond of you."

"Yes, I've known both him and his sister, Gwen, for years. I'll have to introduce you to Gwen, you'd like her, too. We went to high school together, and it was Gwen who told me all about Jesus. Gwen and Garrett are twins, and they've been Christians ever since I've known them. In fact, they both made their decision to follow Christ in their early teens. And Gwen is single."

"That's nice." While it was great that her friend had led Molly to the Lord, he didn't want to meet another woman. It unexpectedly bothered him that she was so anxious to introduce him to her single friend. He'd met the woman of his dreams. Now all he had to do was convince Molly that he was the man of her dreams.

She smiled at his offhanded comment, which did strange things to his insides, and he never wanted it to stop. If this was what is was like to be in love, he liked it.

"I know you probably have a lot of stuff to go through on the quarterly reports, but it would be a real shame for you to have to miss Bible study two weeks in a row. Actually more, because when you were going to take me to your uncle's church's study, it was canceled. You must be catching up to some degree. You don't think you'll have to work overtime again, do you?"

"No, that was a special project." Not that he had anything better to do, except for Wednesday nights. But he hoped that would soon change.

"That's good. I'll bet you haven't had a chance to go out and do much besides work since you got here. Have you had a chance yet to go out and see the sights and get familiar with the city or meet anyone?"

"No, not really."

"Oh, that's too bad. It's really a beautiful place to live. With the mountains to the north and living in the flat Fraser River valley, I think Vancouver is one of the most beautiful places on Earth to live. But of course I can say that, I've lived here all my life and haven't had the chance to see much else except for pictures in magazines and stuff."

"I generally travel only as far as I can go on my bike." Of course, for him and his friends, that was usually a round-trip of eight hundred miles and took about a month.

She laughed and scrunched her nose, which was even more adorable than her usual shining smile. Ken wished he had a camera to keep the moment with him until the end of time. As it was, he thought he could sit and listen to her musical voice forever.

"That's still more than me. I haven't done any traveling. The farthest I've been from here is Kamloops. But it's a beautiful drive. Not that I was driving. It was when I was a teenager and my parents were driving. I suppose you have to travel light when everything you needed was on your bike or your back. Did you at least take a camera?"

Ken wondered why Molly was so talkative. While she did tend to talk a lot whenever they went out together, she'd never chattered so incessantly before. In a way it was both comforting and frightening that he was able to follow her conversation, even though he couldn't remember for the life of him where the discussion had started. "Yes, I take my camera. When I finish a roll of film, I mail it home so it's all waiting for me when I get back. We keep the load as light as possible."

Molly poured herself another cup of coffee from the decanter on their table. "I love to take pictures. I once got an honorable mention in a photo contest. Isn't that neat?" She grinned ear to ear and took another sip, holding the cup to her lips as she waited for him to respond.

Ken frowned. Maybe she'd had too much coffee and that was what was making her so hyper. He wished he could find out what time it was. Since they'd arrived he'd lost track of how much coffee she'd consumed, but it had been a lot, and they hadn't been there that long. In addition to what she'd had at church, he didn't think it was a good idea for her to drink any more if it was going to affect her like this.

He tried to be discreet, but he couldn't read the time on Molly's watch and didn't want to ask. On the way home from work on Monday, he was going to buy himself a wristwatch with an expansion bracelet so he could get it on and off without needing assistance with the clasp like a three-year-old. He glanced around the restaurant, but there wasn't a clock on any of the walls. By the time he looked at Molly again, she was staring at him, probably waiting for him to respond to her last question, which he had to struggle to remember.

"I'd like to see that picture. Did you save it?"

Her head bobbed up and down so rapidly her hair bounced. Ken decided he was definitely going to cut her off the coffee.

"Yes!" Molly exclaimed. "It's the one hanging above my futon. That sunset picture. I took it at Stanley Park."

"Ah. Stanley Park. It's mentioned in much of the tourist literature."

Her hand shot across the table so fast it startled him. She clasped her fingers around his wrist and broke out into another wide smile. "You mean you haven't been to Stanley Park yet?"

"Uh, no."

"Would you like to go? There's lots of great stuff to see and do there. There's totem poles and lots of fields, trails, the zoo, the aquarium. . . It's even got a couple of beaches. I've never swam in the ocean; it's too cold for me, but lots of people do."

It was perfect. Not only could he get her away from the restaurant's bottomless coffee pot, but it was a way to spend the rest of the day with her. "That sounds interesting. Sure. Let's go."

❧

Molly smiled, trying not to show her relief to have something to do besides talk. She'd talked so much she could feel an annoying rasp in her throat, and because of that, she'd drank far too much coffee. She hadn't meant to talk Ken's ear off, but ever since they'd left church he'd been looking at her funny, and she didn't know what to make of it. Every time conversation lagged, a strange half smile appeared on his face, but he didn't say anything; he just stared at her. In the intimate setting of the restaurant, she couldn't stop herself from jumping in to fill the voids in the conversation. At least if they went sightseeing in a crowd, they could just watch the attractions without needing to fill every moment of silence.

Within the confined quarters of the car, she couldn't stop herself from telling him about all the local tourist hot spots. By the time they parked the car, she was tired of listening to herself, and she suspected Ken was, too. As expected, he hadn't said much, but then she hadn't exactly given him a chance. She wouldn't have been surprised if he thought she was some kind of nutcase, but she couldn't stand any silence between them.

Rather than give him a choice, Molly led him to the animals rather than the aquarium complex. Molly wanted to go to the petting zoo, even though it was designed for children. The last time she'd come to the petting zoo she'd taken a friend's child, just so she could go into the pens with the animals and not look foolish. Today she didn't care.

Once inside the enclosure, she headed straight for the feed dispenser and popped in a few quarters to get a handful of the animal chow. She didn't think Ken would feed the baby sheep and llamas even if he did have two hands, but she had no such hesitations. She enjoyed petting the baby animals. She could hardly wait until she could afford a house of her own so she could get a dog. Until then, the petting zoo would have to do.

"Uh, Molly, we're the only adults that are in here without children."

"Don't worry. They won't notice. Besides, they make money from people buying food for them. Think of it as a fundraiser."

At his lack of response, Molly bent down to offer some food to one of the smaller goats who seemed to be left out when the larger and more aggressive animals got ahead of it.

Her next favorite was the tall llama, and after that, she stuck her hand into the pen for the small Vietnamese potbellied pig, a little black fellow whose imaginative name the sign showed as Porky. At first little Porky was hesitant, but once he got up enough nerve, he enjoyed the food she offered.

"Ken, come here. Pat him, he really likes it. Have you ever touched one before? His hair is really strange. It's bristly, but not unpleasant."

"I can't say I've ever patted a pig. I think I'll pass."

She scratched the little fellow behind the ear. He closed his eyes and leaned into her hand.

"I'll bet your name isn't really Porky," she whispered to the little pig. "I'll bet it's something very suave, like Black Bart or something, isn't it?"

"Molly? Are you talking to that pig?"

"Don't worry. He's not answering."

Molly turned to look at Ken over her shoulder to add further to her comment, but before she could say what she intended, the large llama appeared behind Ken. No doubt hoping for some food, it lowered its head and nudged Ken in the back. Unfortunately, he hadn't been expecting it. The llama pushed him forward, causing Ken to stumble. His right arm flew up as he attempted to regain his balance, but with the other arm in the cast, he couldn't right himself quickly. He grabbed hold of the wooden siding for the pen and managed to stay upright, but barely.

Molly stood as quickly as she could. Since the llama had once done that same thing to her, she would have expected it, but she suspected Ken had never been inside a petting zoo in his life. Some of the animals did tend to get aggressive, and she knew from experience that he would be head-butted again. The last thing she wanted was to embarrass him.

"Come on, I've said hello to all my favorites. Let's go somewhere else. How about the aquarium?"

Before he had a chance to reply, Molly grabbed his hand and pulled him out.

eleven

Clicking computer keys, clattering calculators, the whirring of the photocopier, and the electronic tones of ringing phones surrounded Ken. Ignoring everything and remaining seated, he used his foot to push his chair away from his desk and arched to stretch his back. He was on the verge of completing another project, and it felt good.

He couldn't type properly or write yet, but at least he could finally operate the mouse half decently. Most importantly, he could now hold a pen firmly enough to sign his name if he angled the cast properly and leaned crookedly. With this newly acquired skill, his next step would be to sign the lease papers on a new car.

He closed his eyes and drew in a deep breath as he lifted his left arm then rested the cast on top of his head to support the weight while he arched his back again and flexed his aching shoulder. It was the only way to ease the stiffness out, which was driving him nuts after keeping it immobile for so long. Fortunately, from his position at the rear of the office, no one could see him, if anyone had any mind to pay attention to what he was doing. He didn't know how he was going to stand much more of this, but he didn't have any choice. On top of everything else, just as his doctor had predicted, it was starting to get itchy in there.

Out of the corner of his eye, he sneaked a peek at Molly, who was working very hard to convert the labor costs on another project proposal. All thoughts of work fled his mind.

Sitting in his chair, leaning back with his arm still resting on top of his head, he watched Molly. He'd seen so many different facets of her personality yesterday, and it had only served to strengthen how he felt about her.

The woman who had grabbed him by the hand and forcefully pulled him out of the petting zoo had burst into tears over the simple but meaningful words of a children's song. The woman who had charmed his company's most important client had talked to a pig. He didn't want to compare her one-sided conversation with the little animal to his own rather one-sided conversation with her at lunch. Then, for a complete turnaround, instead of a diet of nonstop chatter, during their journey through the aquarium they'd shared a very comfortable silence as they walked slowly through the complex.

Since it had been busy, at one point he had held on to her hand so they wouldn't become separated in the crowd. When the crowd thinned, he hadn't let go, and Molly hadn't pulled away. They'd spent much of their visit walking around the exotic fish and aquatic displays hand in hand, and he'd thoroughly enjoyed himself. The aquarium had been interesting, but being with Molly in the dark complex lit only by the backlight from the aquariums made it enchanting.

The only thing that would have made a great day perfect would have been if he could have kissed her when he left.

He was completely and totally in love with Molly. Now if only he could figure out what to do about it.

He'd never seen an employee out of the working environment before, much less dated one. The situation called for extreme caution, because he didn't want to place Molly in an awkward position in front of his uncle or the rest of the staff. Still, he had every intention of pursuing this as a serious relationship. He'd already kissed her and she'd responded, so he didn't fear that whatever it was they shared wasn't mutual, at least to some degree.

Suddenly, Molly turned her head and looked at him, catching him staring at her. He should have felt stupid leaning back in his chair with his arm on top of his head, but he didn't. Her beautiful emerald green eyes opened wide, her mouth gaped slightly, she stared up at his arm, then quickly reverted her gaze back to his eyes. For lack of a better idea, he smiled at her and said nothing.

She lowered her voice so no one else in the area could hear. "Ken? Is everything all right?"

His smile widened. "Just fine. It's almost lunchtime. Want to beat the rush?"

ᴥ

In the silence of her apartment, Molly slowly spooned a serving of beef stew out of the slow-cooker and onto her plate, then stood and stared at it.

Something strange was happening, and she didn't know what to do. This afternoon she had looked over at Ken to ask him a question, but Molly couldn't believe what she was seeing. The question she was going to ask disappeared in a puff of smoke. Ken had shed his suit jacket and was lounging back in his chair doing absolutely nothing. His tie was loosened around his neck, the sling hung empty, and his arm was raised straight up with the cast lying on the top of his head. And then when he saw her looking at him, all he did was wiggle his fingers and grin like an idiot.

She hadn't expected Ken to take her out for lunch again; after all, they'd had no urgent business to discuss and no important clients to visit. They'd left ahead of the rest of the staff, but once inside the car, she took advantage of the only private moment they were going to have. Ken was careful with his appearance and hated to look unkempt, even to the extent of his tie being crooked. For however long he'd been sitting in that ridiculous position with his arm on top of his head, he'd flattened his hair in the middle. In addition to looking silly with crooked hair, she couldn't look at him with a straight face because the flat spot reminded her of how it got that way. Not only that, if he went out in public like that, he would have been embarrassed.

Therefore, she'd attempted to fix it. And that had been a mistake.

She'd never forget the silky feel of his thick hair as she ran her fingers through it in her efforts to fluff it back up again. While she knew men used hair gel to keep it in that particular style, it was never something she'd used herself. She'd been surprised at the stiffness of it on top, and she couldn't help but investigate the texture of it and experiment with a couple of the hardened strands.

At some point he had closed his eyes, and while she was busy trying to figure out the texture and shaping of his hair, another sappy grin had drifted onto his face. When her fingers stilled, his eyes opened halfway. The usual steel blue had darkened to a blue-gray, and his attention fixed on her mouth. If they hadn't heard the voices of a couple of women leaving the building, she wondered if he would have kissed her.

Molly stared at her supper, which was now starting to cool, and she hadn't taken a single bite. She wasn't hungry, but she knew she should eat. Just as she reached for the cutlery drawer, the buzzer for the door sounded.

"Hi, Molly. It's me, Ken. Are you busy?"

Molly stared at her untouched supper. Not that she was hungry anyway. "No, I'm not busy. What are you doing here?"

"I forgot my tie yesterday and was wondering if I could come up and get it."

Sure enough, his tie was still draped over the kitchen chair where she'd tossed it Sunday morning. "Come on up," she said as she pushed the button to open the main entrance.

Since she hadn't touched her supper, she scraped the stew back into the pot, stirred it, and put the lid back on. By the time she rinsed the plate and tucked it into the dishwasher, Ken was knocking on the door.

"Hi." He stood grinning in the entranceway. "I hope you don't mind. I was just in the neighbor. . . Wow, what's that delicious smell? I hope I'm not interrupting your dinner."

Molly shrugged her shoulders. "I haven't eaten yet."

He craned his neck to look into the kitchen, which fortunately was tidy. "Me neither."

That was a hint if she'd ever heard one. "You're welcome to stay. There's plenty." She'd planned to divide it up into a number of servings and freeze it. While she tended not to be very organized, when it came to suppers, she could do that much. Besides, it saved her from having to cook some other day.

"That would be great. I'm starving. I owe you big time."

"Don't tell me you were at work all this time?"

He shook his head. "No. I was held up with the insurance agent. I got a new car today. Want to go for a test drive?"

"You bought a car? In one day?"

"I knew what I wanted, and I didn't exactly buy it. It's leased. That way I get to claim it on my income tax." He closed the door behind him and walked into the kitchen. "Can I help with anything?"

"No, there's nothing to do." She pulled out a couple of plates and cutlery, poured two glasses of milk, and sat down. In the same space of time, Ken picked up his wayward tie, awkwardly folded it as best he could, and tucked it into his shirt pocket. He shucked off his suit jacket but didn't remove the tie he was already wearing, and after a short prayer, they began to eat.

"This is delicious. You're a good cook."

Molly felt herself blush. "I dumped a bunch of stuff into the pot this morning and turned it on. That doesn't take a lot of effort or imagination. I didn't even have to get up much earlier than usual."

"So did you get the recipe out of a cookbook, or did you just make it up?"

"Make this up? Me? Are you kidding? It was in the book that came with the slow-cooker. I followed the instructions." Molly couldn't believe she was discussing cooking techniques with him. As she shared her limited knowledge of cooking skills, then listened to some cute stories of his misadventures of cooking for one, she had to smile. Perhaps she had the wrong impression, and all Ken had in mind was mere friendship. He hadn't wanted to kiss her after all. Probably her lipstick was smudged, and he didn't know what to say.

She didn't want to be disappointed, but it was best in the long run. Whatever his final position in the company ended up being, it would still be an executive capacity, after all, he was a Quinlan. She'd never be able to relate to his friends or his lifestyle. Most likely, despite her dreams of promotion, all she would ever be was the receptionist, a job she enjoyed but wished paid better.

Instead, she looked for something positive about her discovery concerning Ken's interest. As a friend, he would certainly help her learn about her Christianity. Since she was in his presence all day long, she had the perfect opportunity to ask him any question at any time, rather than having to wait and ask Robbie or Gwen. Not only that, but she could also watch him and learn from his example how he dealt with people, both in business and friendship, being a longtime Christian. It was perfect.

"Thank you for a lovely dinner. Now how about if I take you out for a drive? You can show me some noteworthy points of interest to us tourist types, and I'll treat you to coffee and dessert."

It was a deal she couldn't refuse.

He didn't say anything about the car, but without a doubt, it was priced well beyond her own means, leased or not. Since they'd already been through Stanley Park, she directed him to the outlying areas.

"You'd mentioned something about the SkyTrain and a marketplace a few weeks ago. I don't have any plans for Saturday. Can I take you up on it this weekend?"

She hadn't remembered specifically saying she volunteered to play tour guide, but she couldn't say no without looking churlish. Besides, now that she knew his intentions, she could relax in his company, knowing friendship was all he sought. "Sure. Wear comfortable shoes. We'll be doing a lot of walking."

"Comfortable shoes? Is there any other kind?"

Molly gritted her teeth. She had a closet full of shoes to match every outfit she owned, and then some. And there weren't many in the pile that she'd select to walk for hours at the crowded marketplace.

Instead of describing the points of interest out the window, Molly turned to face Ken as he drove. He obviously didn't have a clue about women's shoes, which was evidenced by his reaction to the spikes she'd worn to the Chamber dinner. And as many suits as he appeared to own, their primary hues were all in very basic, functional, and boring colors. "Just how many pairs of shoes do you own?" she asked, crossing her arms and narrowing her eyes.

His brows knotted as he turned the corner. "Four. If you count my boots and my sneakers. How many pairs of shoes does a person need?"

She could see it in her mind's eye. Basic black, basic brown, white sneakers, and felt-lined boots for a person living in a snowbound winter climate. Exactly four. He didn't even have to think about it. "Oh. . . You're such a. . .a. . . ," she paused and waved one hand in the air, "a man!"

He blinked. "Is that bad?"

"Typical male," she grumbled.

"Well. Excuse me."

Molly cringed at his sarcastic response. She did mean to razz him, but she hadn't meant to insult him. She opened her mouth to apologize, but as he turned his head, his little grin caused her heart to skip a beat and start up in double-time.

"You're teasing me!" she huffed and stared out the window again.

"Me?" He had the nerve to laugh. "Never."

"That does it. We've seen enough of the landscape. You

owe me dessert. And it had better be something chocolate."

ঌ

"Thank you all for coming. I'll see you all again this time next month."

Molly closed her notebook and stood as the Board of Directors did the same. She'd never been to an executive meeting, and she could sum it all up in one word. Dull. Although nothing could have been worse than the mayor's speech at the Chamber of Commerce dinner.

She'd tried her best to take good notes, but out of the corner of her eye, she'd seen that Ken had also taken some notes of his own. To anyone who was watching, it wouldn't have looked strange to see Ken writing with his right hand, but Molly knew better.

Once they had returned to their desks, Molly wheeled her chair beside him, and immediately explained what she had written down, just in case he couldn't understand her writing or had questions.

"I saw you writing, too. What kind of notes were you taking?"

"Nothing," he mumbled. "Did you write down Malcom's question? I can't remember now exactly what he said, but I do know that whatever it was, I thought he had a good point and I wanted to take it up with Uncle Walter later."

Molly paged through her notes, then pointed to the correct spot. "Right here."

He nodded as he read, and while his attention was on her notes, Molly sneaked a peek at his. It was a single page, which he had pushed to the far side of his desk. But she could see it anyway.

There were only a few words on the paper, and they were printed in a large and almost illegible scrawl.

"That's great. I wasn't sure if you caught that. And what about. . ." His voice trailed off as he looked up and saw where she was looking. His mouth snapped shut, and he grabbed the paper, crumpled it up with one hand, and aimed for the garbage can.

Molly grabbed it out of his hand before he threw it. "No, wait, let me see that. It wasn't too bad." Before he could protest, she smoothed it out in front of her.

"I couldn't believe it. I couldn't write with the wrong hand—it was all I could do to print—and as it was, I struggled to do just a few words. It took so much of my concentration for each individual letter that I lost track of the meeting. It was like I was back in kindergarten."

Molly giggled. "I'll bet you were a cute kid in kindergarten."

He tried to snatch the paper, but Molly slapped her hand on top of it.

"I was funny-looking and everyone laughed at me because I was the only one wearing glasses."

"Glasses?"

"Yes, glasses. I wore glasses from a very early age."

"You wore glasses as young as kindergarten?" Molly leaned closer to study his eyes. His gorgeous deep blue eyes. "I've never seen you in glasses. And you're not wearing contacts."

"I had that new laser surgery about a year ago." He grinned wide. "No more glasses. What a difference, huh?"

She didn't know what to say. She had never seen him in glasses, so she couldn't tell. But he was mighty good-looking without them. He was probably just as handsome with glasses; in fact, they would probably add a touch of dignity, since he was an executive. Not liking where her thoughts were headed, Molly returned her concentration to the paper in front of her.

"I think my notes are fairly comprehensive."

"You've done a good job, as usual, and we're nearly done. How would you like to join me for dinner? I'm on my own tonight and have no intention of cooking."

"Sorry. I've got something all defrosted. I'm cooking supper at home."

"Oh."

He looked so dejected, she couldn't help but feel guilty, although she didn't know why. Molly sighed. "Would you like to come over for supper?"

His sullen expression changed instantly into a hopeful smile. "That sounds great. We should be finished soon. I'll follow you home."

Molly tried not to groan.

twelve

Ken followed Molly very carefully. Not only did she take a few shortcuts only the locals would have known about, but her driving was rather erratic. He'd already noticed that the population of the area in general tended to drive too fast and follow too close, to say nothing of aggressive tendencies, but it surprised him to see that Molly was no different.

He sighed and reminded himself not to be judgmental and that most likely after a few years of living here his own driving habits would change and he soon would be no different.

Her poor driving habits aside, Ken felt a strange satisfaction to know that even though they were in separate vehicles, they were headed for the same destination. Molly's home. He smiled to himself as he dreamed about the possibility of one day being in the same car, driving home together after a long day at the office.

His original plan to buy a house shortly after his arrival had changed. At first, the delay was only due to the cast as there was no way he was going to be unpacking with one arm. Now, however, he had no desire to buy a house because he would have been buying it alone. When the cast was off and he could move out of Uncle Walter and Aunt Ellen's house, he had decided to rent something instead. He wondered what it would be like to buy a home with Molly at his side, permanently.

Molly waited for him as he found a spot in the visitor parking, and she complained about the traffic the entire trip up to her apartment. He didn't think he needed to add anything; she said it all, and then some.

The apartment was considerably less tidy than the last time he'd visited, but he had a suspicion, which was further evidenced after observing the condition of her desk day after day, that what he saw of her home today was closer to its usual state than what he'd previously witnessed. He thought that Molly would probably appreciate a housekeeper more than most people.

"Is there something I can help you with, since you didn't expect to be cooking for two?"

She shook her head as she washed her hands in the kitchen sink, then wiped her hands on the dishtowel. "No, you probably wouldn't be that much help anyway." Her hands froze. "I mean, with only one hand what could you do?" Her face flushed red. "I mean, no, I don't want any help."

Ken bit his lip. He'd always know exactly where he sat with Molly. Since she treated him with nothing but open honesty, he could simply relax and be himself, and he hoped she was equally as relaxed in his company.

Rather than go into the living room to sit on the couch by himself, he pulled out one of the kitchen chairs and sat down so they could talk while she prepared supper. He watched as she bustled about the kitchen, and for one of the rare times since they had met, she was silent, probably because she was following the instructions on the box. Her back was toward him as she worked.

It felt rather domestic, and he liked it. His preference would have been to help her, and when he was out of the cast, he hoped to do that someday. His thoughts drifted to the picture of both of them tidying up the kitchen after supper, of washing and drying dishes together, as a couple. The next addition to the domestic picture in his mind was the addition of children and a dog or two.

Ken rested one elbow on the table and leaned his chin into his palm as he slouched forward, still watching Molly. She held the lid above the saucepan, whose contents were now simmering, while she stirred.

"Have you ever thought about getting married?" he asked.

The metal lid crashed down, landing askew on the saucepan

and tottering a few seconds until Molly straightened it. She turned to face him. "Married?" She shrugged her shoulders. "I guess so. When the right man comes along."

"Tell me about your Mr. Right."

Molly turned the heat down and stared at him like he was from outer space. "You want to hear about my Mr. Right? The man of my dreams I haven't met yet?"

According to him, she'd met the man of her dreams, all right. She just didn't realize it yet. He merely had to convince her of it. "Yes. Tell me about the qualities you want to find in your life's mate."

Molly crossed her arms over her chest, tilted her head, scrunched one eye, stuck the tip of her tongue out the corner of her mouth, and looked up to the ceiling as she considered it, then turned to him. "Well, he'd have to be a Christian."

Ken smiled. So far so good. "And then?"

Molly's eyes glazed over, her expression became dreamy, and she turned to study a blank spot on the wall. "No matter what, he's got to love me the same way I love him. Like, totally nuts about each other. Not love at first sight, I don't believe in that. Like best friends, but with a major spark. You know. Romantic stuff. And we'd both be in love totally and completely, faithfully, till death do us part, and all that rot."

Ken smiled. He couldn't have said it better himself, although he would have worded it differently.

Molly sighed. "A good job would help. But it wouldn't really matter, as long as he's ambitious and motivated. I expect to continue working. I don't even care if I made more money and became the major income provider. I took some business courses at night school; I plan to work my way up." She stopped staring at the wall and made eye contact. Her dreamy smile made Ken's chest tighten. All he could do was keep listening.

"You remember the pianist at church? The pregnant one, not the one with the little boy and the puppies. Jillian's a piano teacher, and she's supporting both of them while her husband goes to college. He's going to be a teacher or some-thing, I forget exactly. I wouldn't even mind doing that, either. Supporting my husband while he pursues his life's dream. I think it's kinda sweet. I don't even care what he did, as long as he was happy doing it."

After Ken's cast came off, Uncle Walter was going to make the announcement that Ken was to be named as vice presi-dent of Quinlan Enterprises. That would begin the five-year transition leading to Uncle Walter's retirement, and then Ken would take over as company president. Of course Uncle Walter would still be honorary chairman because he owned the company, but Ken was going to effectively run the entire corporation. That was why he went to college and he'd excelled at all the courses he needed. When he started work-ing for Quinlan Enterprises, he'd started at the bottom and worked his way up, not simply taking over because of his name. He'd worked, and he'd worked hard because he had to prove his worth—that he wasn't being given preferential treat-ment because he was family. The respect he received from the employees was well deserved. He'd earned it the hard way.

Now everything was coming to fruition. Over the next five years, he was going to put both his experience at the working level and all his administrative knowledge into practical application. It was what he'd wanted to do from the time he graduated from high school. He wondered if that qualified as "a good job."

He smiled. "And then what?"

Molly tilted her head and rested one finger on her cheek as she thought for a few seconds. "I wouldn't care what he looked like. I mean, it would be nice if he was good-looking, but what's in the heart is so much more important. I hate it when you meet someone who is so good-looking they're stuck on themselves."

While Ken knew he wasn't the most handsome man to grace the face of the earth, he tried to take care of himself, and he was careful with his appearance, doing the best he could with what God gave him.

"And he should be able to hold his own in a conversation and stand up for himself." Molly's cheeks reddened and her voice lowered. "I sometimes tend to dominate a conversation."

"No!" Ken exclaimed, trying to feign shock. "Really?"

She stuck her tongue out at him and turned away. For once, she didn't comment. Ken laughed.

"What about kids?" he asked, ignoring her silence. Besides, he knew it wouldn't last. "Do you want to have kids?"

Molly nodded. "Of course. A nice house in the suburbs, 2.4 children, the white picket fence. I want it all!" She raised both hands in the air and twirled in a circle, the picture of glee, then turned back at him, smiling ear to ear. She lowered her hands and shrugged her shoulders. "I guess that's about it. What about you? Do you want to get married someday?"

Ken smiled. Not only did he want to get married, he wanted to get married soon, and he knew exactly to whom. "Yes, I do."

That same dreamy expression appeared on Molly's face. She dropped herself into the chair opposite the table from him, rested her elbows on the table, and cupped her chin in her palms. "Tell me about your Miss Right."

He looked straight at Molly. "She'd have to be a Christian."

"Yeah. I figured that. And?"

"Like you, I'd marry for love, nothing else. And if the perfect person didn't come along, I'd stay single."

Molly didn't say anything, so he took advantage of it and continued.

"My position at Quinlan Enterprises is obviously stable, so it's not important to me if the woman I marry works or not. If she wants to work, fine. If not, I'd like her to be involved in some kind of ministry function. Or maybe church secretary if that's what she wanted, and that could be a volunteer position, because we'd be able to afford it."

"You seem to have things pretty mapped out."

He smiled. "No, not really. Those were just a few ideas. I'd also want to be part of a team in some form of ministry. We're talking future dreams here, not necessarily reality, right?"

She shrugged. "I guess so. What else? What would she be like?"

He knew that without hesitation. She'd have untamable red hair and smoky green eyes, be bold and lively, never lack for cheerful conversation, and have a smile that lit the room. "Looks aren't important. What's important is what's underneath. Intelligence, ambition. Waiting for her Mr. Right, which would be me."

Molly scrunched her eyebrows and cocked her head to one side. "Waiting?"

Ken cleared his throat. "Uh, you know. Not, promiscuous."

"I would think that most women aren't promiscuous. It's just that you see so much news about those that are, but really, it's not the norm."

"I know that. But I don't know how many women are waiting for marriage nowadays."

"Waiting for marriage?" Her voice trailed off. He could see the exact second she put two and two together. "Oh!" She snorted rather indelicately and laid both palms on the tabletop. "You know that really bugs me? Men expect that of a woman, but when the shoe is on the other foot, it's different."

Ken stiffened and leaned back in his chair. "Not always."

Molly snorted again.

Ken rested his free hand on top of the cast, the closest he could come to crossing his arms while his mobility was so restricted. What he expected was not unreasonable, nor was it impossible. He was ready to let the subject pass when Molly's mouth dropped open, she leaned toward him and stared deeply into his eyes. At her scrutiny, his face heated up.

"Well, maybe not always, but. . ." She leaned closer, never wavering from a stern eye contact. Her eyes widened and her brows raised. "You've never. . ."

Now his ears burned, too. It was a subject he felt strongly about, but he had never discussed it with another living soul, especially a woman.

"You're saving yourself for marriage! That's so sweet!"

What he really wanted to do was cover his face with his hands, but since he had the use of only one arm, he bent his head forward, pinched the bridge of his nose, and shook his head. He was twenty-seven years old, graduated near the top of his class in college, and was about to become vice president of a major corporation. He had always been an active member of his church and took God's word about love and marriage and chastity very seriously. For all his commitment to doing his best to follow God's direction about avoiding temptation, the last thing he would have been expected to be called was *sweet*.

When he looked up, she was still staring at him. Molly placed one hand on his shoulder. "You know, just because a woman hasn't been a Christian all her life doesn't mean she would give herself away. There are lots of women out there who are waiting, you know."

He didn't know if she was speaking in general terms or if she was speaking of herself. He was afraid to ask.

Molly backed up a bit. "And what about kids? Do you want kids?"

Ken cleared his throat. "Yes, I want kids. I'm an only child, and even though we had a large extended church family, I always wanted brothers and sisters. Or even a cousin would have been nice. When I get married, I want kids. I never thought about how many. Just more than one."

"I have one brother. But when I was a kid, I wished I had a dog instead."

He allowed himself to relax, since the conversation was drifting onto more comfortable territory. "I had a dog when I was a boy. I'd like a dog, too. But I wouldn't allow my daughter to call it Missykins."

Molly giggled. "Me neither!"

Ken smiled. "Well, I guess that makes us a perfect match, don't you think?"

She laughed out loud, which made Ken doubt she took him

seriously, even though he'd never been more serious in his life. Obviously the light touch wasn't going to work.

The timer for the stove dinged. Molly spooned some kind of ground beef and pasta mixture onto two plates. "Another famous gourmet meal. Just read the instructions on the box."

It took Ken a few seconds to realize that she was comparing it to the recipe for the stew they'd had yesterday.

After a few words of thanks, they began to eat. Ken had never eaten anything like this in his life, but it wasn't bad, considering.

"Even you could do this, you know, even with one hand."

"Naw," he mumbled. "I'd prefer you to do it for me."

Molly choked on her mouthful.

Ken rapidly shook his head. "I didn't mean I want you to cook for me. I meant that I enjoy your company and that includes mealtime. I'd cook for you if I could. In fact, when I'm out of the cast, I'd love to cook a meal for you." If that's what it took, he'd do anything.

She mumbled something he couldn't hear, and he didn't dare to ask her to repeat herself.

Fortunately he managed to steer the conversation after that to less personal territory. After dinner, he would have liked to help her do the dishes but didn't want to take the chance of dropping anything. Rather than allow him to watch her clean up the kitchen, Molly shooed him into the living room. He heard everything getting piled into the sink, and before he knew it, she joined him on the futon.

With a flick of the remote, she turned on the television, and they enjoyed a few programs, interspersed with much conversation. The domesticity of it all appealed to him, and he wanted more.

Now to figure out how he was going to achieve that.

thirteen

Molly studied the spreadsheet on her computer, then wrote down a few notes so she could remember how she figured out her latest entry. She knotted her eyebrows as she studied the endless statistical data, absently winding the pencil through her hair as she read. She was so lost in thought that when the phone at her elbow rang, she jumped. The pencil tangled in her hair, and when she pulled it out, it caught in her earring. A ping clicked in her ear as the earring unfastened and flew into the air. The pieces bounced off the edge of the desk, fell to the floor, and rolled under her desk.

"Molly speaking. May I help you?" she mumbled into the phone as she tried to see where her earring had went. "Hmmm. . . ," she mumbled as she tipped her head to the side, trying to look under her desk at the same time as she listened to Janice's questions. "Oh. That. It's in the second drawer in the folder marked 'Correspondence.' Yeah. You're welcome. Bye."

The second she hung up, she pushed her chair back, bent at the waist, and continued to check farther underneath the desk. She found the main piece of the earring easily, but the small back fastener was nowhere to be seen. A small glint caught her eye, so she dropped to her hands and knees and crawled under her desk to retrieve the missing piece. It ended up being only a broken shard of something she couldn't identify, but since she was already on the floor, she remained under the desk to try to locate it. Not only were they her favorite earrings, they were a gift from Gwen.

Voices drifted from above the desk as footsteps approached. "Surprise, surprise. They're both gone again."

"And it isn't even lunchtime."

"Why do some women have all the luck? What's she got that I ain't got?"

"Ken Quinlan, that's what."

"How in the world did she do it?"

"Take a guess, Francine."

The first woman made a disgusted sound and gave a rather rude comment, and the voices faded as they walked away.

Cautiously, Molly backed up, slowly raising her head inch by inch to scan the area to see if anyone noticed her. Everyone in the vicinity sat with their noses glued to their work, so she rose as nonchalantly as she could and sat back in her chair.

Did people really think something was going on between her and Ken?

His chair was empty, but she heard his voice coming from Mr. Quinlan's office.

She hadn't tried to hide the fact that he'd taken her out for lunch on a number of occasions, but she was mortified to hear that the rumor mill had reared its ugly head to make more of things than really happened.

The last thing she wanted was to damage Ken's reputation, or her own. In the future, she would make sure they were not gone at the same time so people with overactive imaginations could no longer weave their tall tales. Naturally she liked Ken. Who wouldn't? But to think that she had any claims on him was ludicrous.

The first time she'd had the mistaken impression that his interest might be other than friendship was the weekend he'd kissed her. As pleasant as it was, afterward he'd obviously thought twice about it, because the next day at work, he'd distinctly told her their relationship would be business only except for Bible or church-related stuff. If he had considered anything other than friendship, it had taken only one day to change his mind.

For a few minutes on Monday she'd wondered what was going on in his head when she caught him watching her with that sappy grin on his face. But when he appeared at her doorstep to get his tie, he had only sightseeing on his mind and that was fine with her. And yesterday, after spilling his guts about his dreams for finding the ideal woman, she knew that what he felt for her was strictly a platonic friendship, otherwise he wouldn't have said such personal things.

When Ken returned to his desk with an armful of papers, Molly took the opportunity to dig out some files she needed from the back room. For the rest of the day, she made sure when she needed something, even if it was only a piece of paper, she fetched it when Ken was busy at his desk, so people could see she wasn't with him. Also, when Ken was gone, she made sure that she spent as much time as she could in plain view of as many people as she could, right at her own desk.

❧

All day long, Ken had the feeling something was wrong. Many times he'd caught Molly sneaking little glances at him, watching him but never saying anything. He would get completely immersed in his work, and then the next time he would look up, she would be gone. If he left to do something, when he got back, there she was, as if she'd been there all along. If he didn't know better, he would have thought she was avoiding him.

The thought terrified him.

The worst part was that he didn't know what he'd done wrong. Sure, he'd laughed at her obsession with shoes, but that was days ago, and besides, he didn't think that was something worth being given the cold shoulder over. Not that she was exactly giving him the cold shoulder, but he couldn't ascertain what was wrong. She'd been fine for most of the morning, but at some point, something changed.

He had to find out what it was.

By the time the work day came to an end, he was a nervous wreck. Sure enough, Molly appeared back at the desk just long enough to tidy up her mess. He saw her open the drawer for her purse, ready to leave. Without him. He couldn't let the sun go down on her anger. Or whatever it was that was bothering her.

"Molly? Could I see you for a minute please? In private?"

Her hand froze, she yanked her purse out of the drawer, slammed it shut, and hugged the purse to her body like a shield. "Now?" Her eyes darted around the room, as if she was searching for someone or something.

Which only confirmed that something was terribly wrong.

"I'm kind of in a rush. Can't you just tell me here?"

His heart clenched. "No. Can you come into Uncle Walter's office?"

Again, she looked skittishly around the room. He felt sick. If he'd done anything to hurt or frighten her, he'd never forgive himself.

He stood tall and walked into his uncle's office, and Molly eventually followed. At a distance. He motioned to the two chairs and closed the door. She remained standing, her posture rigid.

"Molly, please, tell me what's wrong."

"Wrong? Nothing's wrong."

Rather than contradict her, he tried to act calm and wait her out. His stomach clenched when she avoided looking directly at him.

"Okay, I'll tell you what's wrong. Have you picked up on any of the rumors yet?"

"No, I haven't." Relief washed through him. If all that happened was that word was starting to circulate about him being named vice president or taking over Uncle Walter's presidency in five years, then he'd worried for nothing. Even though they didn't want anyone to know until the official announcement was made, he knew that in large organizations sometimes information leaked out. He no longer cared, as long as nothing was wrong between himself and Molly. He wished he could understand why the news had affected her so much that she was now avoiding him, but at least it was something he could deal with. "So?"

"So we shouldn't be going out for lunch so often."

He failed to see why not. Most high-ranking executives with controlling interest had personal secretaries or assistants, and they often lunched together.

"And it's getting worse, you know."

"Worse?"

"Do you want to know what I heard this afternoon?"

"You heard something?"

"I heard a couple of the guys laughing about more than just business going on in the boardroom. And they weren't the only ones talking."

Ken frowned. The employee's personal affairs were their own business, but if employees were using company time for personal liaisons, he would have to follow it up with disciplinary action.

"And now we're in here with the door closed."

"What's that got to do with anything?"

"You don't get it, do you?" She waved one arm in the air, in the other she continued to hug her purse next to her body. "People are spreading rumors that we're having an affair!"

"An affair? That's ridiculous."

Molly sighed loudly. "Tell me about it."

He stepped closer to Molly. The anger in her eyes made them sparkle and it made her cheeks flush. She radiated energy, and her anger spoke righteousness. And he loved her for it. "An affair implies something tawdry and short-lived. Nothing could be further from the truth."

Molly nodded. "You're telling me."

"You're far too valuable for a tawdry affair. You deserve to be courted properly."

"Yeah, and I think—" She gulped, and her eyes widened. "I beg your pardon?"

"Tonight's Bible study. May I take you out for dinner before we go? Oh, didn't you say you were in a rush to go somewhere?"

Her eyes widened even more and her mouth gaped as she stared at him in open astonishment. "Uh. Yeah. Right. I was. Bye."

Before he had a chance to say another word, she turned and ran.

੨

Molly had barely changed into her jeans when the buzzer for the door sounded. She knew who it was. It was Ken, and he was expecting her to go out to dinner with him.

It was probably rude of her to turn and run out on him at the office when he had been expecting a reply about dinner, but his remark had thrown her so off guard, she hadn't known what to do.

She tried to figure out what he meant by courting her properly. They were friends. He was her boss. He probably had millions of women after him, women more in his social and economic circles. Or at least he would, once he got settled and met more people. Was he lonely? Maybe he needed to meet more people. And quickly.

Knocking sounded on the door. She opened it and nearly fainted. Gone was the suit and tie. Ken stood before her in jeans, a casual shirt, and a light jacket.

And he was holding a flower. A single long-stemmed red rose.

He grinned and held the flower toward her. "Hi."

She nearly choked and had to struggle to speak. "Hi, yourself. What is that for?" She tried to convince herself he had merely run into someone selling flowers and had bought it out of an act of charity. It didn't mean anything personal.

"It's for you."

Very delicately, she took the flower from him, scrounged through the cupboards for the only bud vase she owned, and placed it in the middle of the kitchen table. Before she left the room, she inhaled its sweet fragrance. No man had ever given her flowers before, and therefore, she knew she would always treasure this moment. She dreamed of the day a man would give her a flower as more than a kindhearted gesture. One day it would be for romance. But until then, she could dream. Ken simply wasn't her type.

Everything about Molly shouted casual, but Ken was the suit and tie type, although she had to admit he looked fabulous in the jeans. Almost everything she did was spontaneous; Ken had his whole life planned out. He was well on his way to being rich. She. . .wasn't.

"I've got the perfect place in mind for dinner. Really casual. It's always crowded and loud because lots of people take their kids, but the food's great."

Ken smiled, and Molly forgot what else she was going to say. One day, when he did start courting someone, that would be one very lucky woman. And she knew the perfect person.

&

"Ken, I'd like you to meet my friend Gwen."

"Pleased to meet you, Gwen."

"Pleased to meet you, too, Ken."

Molly stifled a giggle. Ken and Gwen. The combination sounded so silly, but there was nothing silly about the way they looked together.

Ken radiated class. Even in the crowded and noisy living room, everything cast aside, he'd still managed to set himself apart. Well mannered and gracious, but not to the point of stuffy, they'd had a wonderful time, until they realized they were nearly late. Gwen had laughed about it while Ken had grumbled something about a cheap watch.

They stood together and chatted. Gwen was slightly taller than Molly, thinner, and with the understated grace of a model. She couldn't help but picture Ken in his usual suit with his usual dignified demeanor. They suited each other.

Just like Ken, Gwen also tended to be quiet and reserved when in a crowd. Gwen had class. Gwen also had hair that behaved and didn't look like she stuck her finger in a light socket every time the weather got a little damp, which in

Vancouver was almost always.

Molly laid a hand on Ken's free arm, then hastily pulled it away when she realized she was touching him. "I've known Gwen for years, and Gwen was one of the people who helped me find Jesus."

He smiled wide. "Ah, yes. I've heard quite a bit about you."

Gwen laughed softly. "I've heard a lot about you, too. We'll have to talk."

Molly watched the two of them smiling at each other. Her own smile began to drop, but she forced it back.

Robbie's voice drifted from the kitchen. "Gwen? Who are you talking to?"

Robbie and Garrett rounded the corner arm in arm. Molly caught them exchanging a glance that made her long for the day someone would look at her like that, and that someday she could be as in love as her friends.

"Oh, Ken, Molly. We didn't hear you come in."

Before she could say anything, the doorbell rang and more people entered. Everyone stood and chatted for a few minutes, then took their seats. Molly quickly sat in Garrett's big armchair, which left Ken to sit beside Gwen.

They shared a number of prayer requests, which included praying for Ken and his broken arm. Molly cringed, as a few of the people there kept looking at her strangely, then stealing glances at him. Before she'd come to know Ken so well, she'd been very distraught as she told the group that she'd been the one responsible for his injury. She had barely managed to not break down and cry in front of them when she asked for prayer for the situation. And now here he was, in person. She didn't know what to make of the way everyone kept looking at them.

Ken seemed not to notice the sideways glances. She forced herself to smile when Ken thanked everyone for their prayers, and they moved on to the topic of their study.

Every once in awhile, she sneaked a peek at Ken and Gwen, sitting side by side. They were comfortable together.

When the study was over, they remained seated, engrossed in conversation while others socialized around them.

Molly squirmed in her chair. Wasn't that what she wanted?

fourteen

Molly told Ken he could just drop her off, but he insisted on escorting her all the way up to her door. Once there, she couldn't very well turn him away, so she invited him in and put the kettle on to boil for tea, since it wasn't that late.

She nearly dropped the teapot when she turned around and saw him standing in the doorway to the kitchen instead of where she left him, sitting on the futon.

"I thought I'd see if I could do anything to help."

"With one hand? I don't think—" Molly slapped her hands over her big mouth. She'd done it again.

"Don't worry, Molly. You don't have to watch what you say around me. I'm a big boy, and I'm fully aware of my limitations. But praise God they're only temporary." He raised the cast slightly and grinned. "And I can still reach the top shelf with my other hand. You can't."

"Very funny."

"It's true."

Molly scowled. "I don't need anything on the top shelf." When Gwen came over, it was Gwen who reached the stuff on the top shelf. Molly busied herself finding the box of tea bags and searched through the cupboards for a bag of cookies that she knew she had somewhere.

"I like your friends. Thank you for inviting me. I guess I'll see them all again on Sunday."

"Yeah." Last week Gwen hadn't been there, but she would be there next Sunday.

He didn't say anything but continued to stand in the doorway, watching.

"I thought you and Garrett would spend all your time talking about camping and the great outdoors."

"I really didn't have a lot of time to talk to him. The evening went so fast."

Molly poured the boiled water into the teapot. "I know," she mumbled, concentrating intently on her aim. "You spent all your time talking to Gwen."

"What did you say?"

She turned the cookie bag upside down and dumped some cookies onto the plate. "Nothing," she muttered under her breath while she shoved the bag back into the cupboard.

"I don't remember you telling me that Garrett and Gwen are twins. That's fascinating. I understand they have a very unique relationship."

She took a spoon and fished the tea bag out of the pot and splatted it in the sink, perhaps throwing it a little too hard. "Yeah."

"Did you know that when they were young, they did a number of magazine ads and even a commercial? It's too bad they didn't have VCRs back then. Gwen said she would have liked to have saved a copy to show her children someday."

Molly slammed the lid onto the teapot. "Well, you spent enough time talking to her. I'm surprised she didn't tell you her life's story."

Instead of turning and walking into the living room, Ken stepped forward. Before she had a chance to start pouring their tea, he rested his fingers on her cheek, drawing her complete attention to his eyes. His beautiful dark blue eyes. Eyes that saw down into her soul. Only inches separated them.

"Mostly, we talked about you."

Her heart started pounding, and she couldn't control it. She wanted to move. She couldn't. "Me?"

His thumb brushed under her chin. Butterflies fluttered in Molly's stomach. She reminded herself to breathe. Ken's voice came out in a deep whisper. "You know what I want to do, don't you?"

He tilted her chin up. The butterflies engaged in battle. She tried to keep her eyes open. She really did. But they drifted closed of their own accord as their lips touched. And she was lost.

❧

Ken kissed Molly, and in so doing, the last remaining reservations of why he shouldn't be doing this were gone. He kissed her gently at first and then with all the love in his heart. He wanted to wrap his arms around her and envelop her completely as he kissed her, but the best he could do was run the fingers of his right hand through her soft silky hair. With his left arm fixed in a forty-five degree angle, he could only touch his fingertips to the side of her waist.

When she raised her arms and wrapped them around his neck, he thought his heart would burst. He was kissing the woman he loved, and she was kissing him back.

It took great restraint to stop. Instead of releasing her completely, he held her until he could let go without it feeling like a piece of him was missing.

"I, uh, think we should go into the living room," Molly said at the same time as she picked up both mugs, now filled with lukewarm tea.

Ken picked up the plate of cookies and followed her, laid the plate on the coffee table, and sat on the left side of the futon. While Molly placed the cups on the table and picked up the remote for the television, Ken patted the seat beside him. "Please sit beside me."

Her eyes widened, but she didn't comment. When she actually did sit beside him, his breath released in a rush, and it was only then he realized he'd been holding it. Without hesitation, he slipped his arm around her until she leaned into him, and he held her in a loose embrace.

The program droned on. It was supposed to be a sitcom, but Ken wasn't paying attention. Molly was warm and comfortable as she leaned against him, settled in for the duration of the show, which he hoped was an hour long. It was very rare for her to be silent for so long, and he hoped it was because she was enjoying the closeness as much as he was.

After about ten minutes, as he knew would happen, Molly was the first to break the silence. She turned and forced direct eye contact while his arm remained around her shoulders. "I thought you just wanted to be friends."

"I do. There's more than one type of friend, you know."

No answer came, and Ken smiled to himself at her lack of response as she settled back in. He could almost hear the gears whirring around in her head. The type of friend he wanted Molly to be was the happily ever after kind. The kind a man wanted as his best friend and helpmate during the day and his lover at night. That one in a million woman, chosen for him by God, to be together for the rest of their lives, the mother of his children. He wanted to marry Molly. But just as he had promised, before he asked for her hand in marriage, he fully intended to court her properly.

By the close of the program, she still hadn't said anything, so Ken thought it was a good time to make a graceful exit. Despite how he wanted to kiss her, he left her at the door with a chaste kiss on the cheek. Now all he had to do was figure out what to do next.

◈

Ken heard her before he saw her. Or rather, he heard a strange hush and a few people calling out her name in greeting as she walked into the office. He knew she was very sensitive to potential gossip concerning his attentions toward her in the office, so Ken tried his best to concentrate on his work and not look up until Molly slid into her chair at the desk beside him.

"Good morning, Molly. And how—" He lifted his head and blinked a few times, but the sight before him didn't change. "What have you done to your hair!?"

A different Molly faced him. The red was gone. Instead of the vivid and lively color he'd come to know and love, it was some kind of lifeless, dull, dark brown. The bounce was also gone. It lay flat and tame and sluggish and in an orderly style. It didn't suit her at all.

He stood and walked the two steps to her desk so he could

speak without the entire office listening in. He did his best to ignore those around who were pretending they weren't watching or straining to hear their every word.

"It's a henna." She shook her head to show it off, and it still didn't bounce. "Do you like it?"

He hated it.

She ran the fingers of both hands through it, and it fell heavily when she let it go. He started to lift his free hand to also run his fingers through it to examine the loss, almost needing to feel it as proof that she'd really done it. At the last second, he clenched his fingers and dropped his hand to his side, remembering they were in plain view of anyone who cared to look. And they were looking.

It finally hit him. Molly was right. He had to be very careful about what he said and did around her. His obvious shock and the way he'd approached her without thinking just proved to the entire office staff that she was more to him than simply a mere employee. If anyone else had done something so drastic with their hair, it might have garnered a raised eyebrow, but nothing more.

When he first met Molly he'd been amazed by the striking color of her hair, but the more he saw of her, it continually fascinated him how she could never get it under control. It enchanted him, just as the woman beneath the wild hair.

"Uh, is it permanent?"

"No, after a few washings it comes out. I think. But it's supposed to be really good for your hair. I'm not sure about the color. What do you think?"

He didn't know very much about women, but there were certain things he knew a man had to be careful about when expressing his opinions. He suspected this was one of them. "I think, uh, that it might be a little. . . ," he struggled to find the right word, "dark."

"Yeah. I did it last night, and I might have used a little too much or left it on too long or something. I'm not sure I did it right, and I don't think I got it all out. But it was really late."

He wondered why in the world she would have stayed up late to play with her hair, which was perfectly fine the way it was. Not that it was late when he left, but when he arrived home at his uncle's house he'd gone straight to bed. He had fallen asleep right away and dreamed of little children with bright red hair.

"There was nothing wrong with your hair."

She ran her fingers through it again. "It never behaves and when it gets damp it gets so wild and frizzy. Don't you ever want to change your hair just for the sake of something different?"

He patted the top of his head. He'd worn it in the same style for years. It looked fine and was easy to care for with regular trips to the salon. "No."

She shrugged her shoulders. "Well, I think I might regret this, but at least I can say I tried it. I'll probably wash it out as soon as I get home from work tonight."

Ken decided that tonight, he would leave her alone. He understood the standard brush-off joke when a woman didn't want to date someone, she would use the excuse that she had to wash her hair. In this instance, it was legitimate. And in this case, he would encourage it.

"I have plans for Friday night, but don't forget that you promised to take me sightseeing on Saturday."

"Oh. Right. Of course. I haven't forgotten."

Rather than give the office more to speculate on, Ken returned his attention to the project on his desk.

He could hardly wait for Saturday.

❧

As soon as Ken pulled up, Molly ran to the car and hopped in. During their excursion to the zoo and aquarium at Stanley Park, they somehow ended up holding hands. At the time she didn't attach too much significance to it since every tank was surrounded by a close crowd and they didn't want to get separated. However, after the way he'd kissed her, claiming some kind of friendship she never dreamed would involve kissing, she wanted to make sure that this time, there would be no opportunity for more of the same.

Today, she was going to take him to the marketplace. Unlike the aquarium, today they would be in bright daylight where it was busy and offered no privacy.

"I'm going to introduce you to the SkyTrain today. We're going to leave your car at the Park-N-Ride. Go that way." She pointed in the right direction.

"Your hair looks nice."

It didn't look any different than normal. She ran her fingers through it, then fluffed it up. "Thanks. I had to wash it a number of times over the past few days, but I got most of the henna out. It's almost back to my natural shade. I guess I'll never do that again. Maybe I'll get it cut instead."

"No!"

Ken's sudden exclamation made Molly jump. She turned to him, and not only did his cheeks turn red, his ears flushed, too. She couldn't remember knowing a man who blushed before, yet again she'd caught Ken doing it. She found the trait rather endearing.

His voice lowered and he cleared his throat. "Of course, it's your decision, but I like your hair the way it is." He turned into the parking lot and found a space.

They walked to the station, bought their tickets out of the machine, and climbed the stairs to the platform to wait for the next SkyTrain.

"I've never been on a monorail before. This should be interesting."

"Thousands of people take it every day. It's part of the regular transit system, no different than a bus, except it's above the ground. And there's no traffic."

The next train approached the station, slowed, and when it came to a stop, the doors whooshed open. Molly led Ken into the nearest car.

"Isn't anyone going to check our tickets?"

"No. It's an honor system. They have random checks.

Someone might come check and see if we have our tickets somewhere along the ride."

They sat down. Electronic chimes sounded to signal the doors closing, and the train started moving.

"How fast does this thing go?"

"I'm not sure. I think up to forty miles an hour. It actually goes pretty fast. And I must admit I was nervous at first with a fully automated system."

"Fully automated?"

"Yes. There's no driver."

Ken's face paled, and Molly wondered if he would bolt, except the car was already in motion. "What do you mean, no driver?"

Molly rested her hand on his shoulder. "Don't worry. It's run by a computer, but they do have people at the main control center. It's always monitored."

"You're serious. There really isn't a driver?" He glanced forward. They were in the center car, and they couldn't see the first car, but Molly knew all the cars were identical, because none required staffing.

She smiled, imagining his reaction to her next statement. "Don't worry. If anything happens, the system simply shuts down."

He looked out the window to the ground, about twelve feet below as they whizzed along. "Then what? Does everyone have to jump?"

"No, everyone just waits until it moves again. There's a radio in every car in case of emergency, see?" She pointed to the unit, clearly marked to be used only in time of emergencies. "And problems don't happen as often as they used to."

"Why doesn't that instill me with confidence?"

Molly couldn't help herself. She laughed. "Relax, I'm teasing you. The technology works really well. Stops between stations are extremely rare. Now enjoy the ride."

He mumbled something under his breath about his perfectly reliable car sitting idle in the parking lot, but Molly couldn't fully understand what he was saying. She decided not to comment further and leaned back in the seat.

As the monorail continued on its path through the city, Molly filled him in about the districts and municipalities they passed through, the points of interest, and then a bit of history as the train went underground at the downtown core of Vancouver. In due time, they arrived at the end of the line where all passengers exited. Most walked to the SeaBus terminal.

Molly didn't take the SkyTrain or the SeaBus often, but had done it enough to know the routine. Having been born and raised in the Vancouver area, she could tell by watching which people were boarding the SeaBus for the first time, observing their first shaky steps as they walked from the solid land onto the floating portion of Vancouver's public transit system as it bobbed slightly in the water. Ken was no different.

Once aboard, she led Ken to the front seats against the window. Molly bit her bottom lip as Ken tried not to look too enthralled with the uniqueness of the next part of their journey. She suspected that if he were younger, his face would have been pressed to the glass, just as the young boys beside them. They passed Stanley Park and the floating fueling stations for boats on the river, past a massive ocean container vessel, then pulled into the docking station in North Vancouver. Most of the crowd traveled from the SeaBus to the market.

"Here we are. The Lonsdale Quay."

He tilted his head back to take in the sprawling three-story complex. "It's huge."

The first section she led him to was the food court, where she stopped to buy her favorite snack. "Try this. It's great." She held the morsel up to his face.

He craned his neck backward. "What is it?"

"I'm not sure what's in it. Mostly seafood mushed up and wrapped in some kind of Oriental-type white stuff."

"No, thanks. I think I'll pass."

Molly popped it into her mouth and savored it, bite by bite. "Coward."

"Yes, but I'm a live coward."

She licked her fingers, then pinched her thumb and index finger together and gave them a loud smacking kiss as she moved her hand away from her mouth. "You don't know what you're missing."

"That's fine with me."

Molly snorted and led him to the next concession.

"You're not buying something else strange to eat, are you?"

"Yup."

After that, Molly led him around the market, which varied from artisans displaying and constructing their wares, curio and souvenir shops, produce, and entrepreneurs selling everything imaginable.

She was about to lead him outside so they could sit on the bench beside the Burrard Inlet and rest their feet for a few minutes before they went to the next level when his hand closed around hers and pulled gently.

"Wait. I want to go in here."

"But that's a toy store."

"I know. Something caught my eye."

As far as Molly could remember, Ken was an only child and did he have any cousins, so she knew he didn't have any nieces or nephews back home. She didn't know who he might want to buy a toy for, but since they'd looked at nearly everything at the marketplace, she allowed him to lead her into the toy store.

He went straight for a rack of stuffed toys, where he dropped her hand and picked out a small fuzzy bear.

He held it up and smiled. "Perfect."

Without another word, he proceeded to pay for it, and they left the store.

Molly led him outside to the bench, flopped down, stretched out her feet while wiggling her toes inside her sneakers, arched her back, then turned to Ken. While she was curious about the bear, she did manage to hold herself back from asking, because it was probably none of her business.

He fumbled with the bag enough to grasp the bottom with the fingers that were sticking out of the cast, reached inside with his free hand, and pulled out the bear. "This is for you." He laid it in her hands, and then to her surprise, he raised his hand and ran his fingers through the bottom strands of her hair. "It's the same color as your beautiful hair. Without the henna."

Molly stared at the cute little bear. In its own little way, it seemed to be smiling at her, almost laughing, if a toy could do such a thing. She tried not to think about the odd color of her hair except when she was buying clothes, and at that time, she usually considered it a curse. When she met new people, the first thing they generally commented on was her flaming, wild hair. To see the same color on a toy was indeed a shock to her system. It looked better on the bear than it did on her.

"I don't know what to say. Thank you."

She lifted her head, but instead of what she expected, his fingers drifted to her chin and he leaned his face close to hers. "You're welcome," he whispered against her lips, then brushed the lightest of kisses to her mouth.

Against her better judgment, she was disappointed when he didn't kiss her again. Instead of sitting back in the chair immediately, he only moved a few inches away, smiled, and maintained eye contact, making her hope he was going to kiss her again despite the public setting. When a noise sounded behind them, Ken leaned back fully on the bench but sustained eye contact. Most important, his contented little smile highlighted the adorable crinkles at the corners of those eyes she was beginning to know and love.

Despite the unusual location, Molly considered what he'd done quite romantic. Acting outside his conservative nature, he surprised her and she was delighted, even though she shouldn't have been.

"Let's get back inside. We made it about halfway through, we still have lots to see."

He never lost his smile, and this time, when Molly stood, Ken reached out for her hand, as if she needed help up, then didn't let go. After the little flutter her heart made when he kissed her, she didn't want to protest, so they continued on to investigate the shops hand in hand.

As they passed a boutique displaying a few souvenir T-shirts in the window, Molly stopped. "Wait. This is what every tourist to Vancouver has to have. I'll bet you don't have anything that says 'Vancouver' on it, do you?"

"Well, I—"

"I didn't think so."

"But I'm not a tourist. I live here now."

"That's beside the point."

Not giving him any opportunity to protest, she pulled his hand and led him into the store, where she saw someone holding one of the shirts up to a light, which was part of the display inside the store. After being exposed to the light, the black and white sketch outline drawing came alive with colors.

Molly shook his hand, just in case he wasn't watching. "Wow, look at that! The shirt changes in the light. Did you see it?"

"That's fascinating. I wonder how it's done?"

Molly yanked one off of the rack and held it up to his chest. "Perfect. Don't move."

Before he had a chance to open his mouth, she rushed off to pay for the T-shirt.

Within a few minutes, Molly returned to Ken and held out the bag toward him. "This is for you. It makes you a proper tourist."

"But I already told you, I'm not—"

She held one finger in the air to silence him. "Consider it an initiation. Everyone has to have a shirt that says 'Vancouver' on it. I've got one, too."

"Thank you, Molly. I don't know what to say."

"Then don't say anything. Come on. We still have lots of stuff to see."

When he reached for the bag, Molly stuffed it into her purse instead. This way, he would have his only available hand free to hold her hand. She didn't want to think of why she wanted it so badly. Monday, when they were back to work, it would be business as usual, but for now, she planned to enjoy herself, which mostly included a good case of the warm fuzzies from being with Ken.

They wandered past all the small shops, but every once in a while, she made sure she led him back to someplace she could buy a snack.

"Don't you ever quit eating?"

Molly finished the last prawn in the bag from her latest purchase and threw the tail in the garbage bin. "This isn't really eating. It's snacking. All the calories I consumed today are canceled by the diet cola."

"I'm not even going to comment."

She also chose not to mention that Ken had consumed a fair amount of food himself, especially considering how much he complained. Even if he protested today, one day, she would get him to eat seafood. "I just want to get one more thing, and I think we'd better head home."

He nodded. "It's probably not a good idea to wander around here after dark, is it?"

"I don't know, but I'd think not. We're a long way from home."

He checked his watch. "Fine by me. Let's head back."

Molly redirected him to the place that sold the little seafood rolls and asked for two, determined this time to at least get him to taste it. To her horror, she discovered that after paying for the T-shirt, she didn't have enough money left in her wallet.

She lowered her voice to a whisper. "Ken, can you do me a favor? Can I borrow some money?"

"I'd be more than happy to buy it for you, Molly."

She shook her head. "No. I want to buy one for you. You've really got to try this. I'll pay you back. I promise."

One side of his mouth quirked up. "Let me get this straight.

You're borrowing money so you can buy me something I have no intention of trying."

Her face flamed. "Something like that."

His laughter rang out, a cheery sound that made Molly's heart beat faster, which was something else she became determined to control. "A deal I can't refuse." Once he paid for the two rolls, the clerk presented them to Molly, and she turned to give one to him.

Molly delved into hers immediately, savoring every bite. Ken stared at his in such a way that she wondered if he had the use of both hands if he would be picking it apart like a little kid before deciding if he was actually going to risk taking a bite.

She nudged him with her elbow, since both her hands were busy. "Taste it. It's really good."

He took the smallest bite known to man, then rolled it around in his mouth before swallowing it almost painfully. "Sorry, but I really don't like seafood." Sheepishly, he handed it back to her.

Molly sighed. "I'm not shy. I love these things." Gustily, she ate Ken's roll, then licked her fingers. "Okay, let's go home."

"I guess we've both eaten so many snacks that stopping for supper is a foolish idea."

Molly nodded and tried to hold back a burp.

fifteen

Molly slid into the seat of the SkyTrain car, and Ken slid in beside her.

"There are far less people going home than on the way here, aren't there?"

"Yes," Molly said. "This is normal for a Saturday. Remember, for most people, this is suppertime."

"We've been sitting here for a long time. Why aren't we moving?"

"The SkyTrain turns around here. See, behind us." Molly pointed to the opening where the switch for the track was, just beyond the wall. "This is where the trip begins eastbound, so the train will just sit here for a few minutes until it's time to go. It's a schedule thing." Molly turned her head, but Ken was looking around the car. He tilted his head back as he read the ads displayed in a neat row along the curved edge of the ceiling of the car.

"Look at that. There's an ad for a 3-D movie. I remember when I was a kid, some cereal box had a 3-D picture on it, and they enclosed the glasses to go with it. I was fascinated by it. I was about nine years old and attempted to draw some 3-D pictures. My mother saved a few, even after all these years. It's harder than you'd think it would be, you know. I can't imagine a whole movie in 3-D."

"You mean you've never been to a 3-D movie before? Are you serious?"

He nodded, then shook his head. "Never."

Molly started to push him out of the seat, forcing him to stand. "You don't know what you're missing. Let's go."

"But we haven't even gone one stop."

"I know. It's right here. Let's go." Molly continued to nudge him until they were both out of the car. "I haven't seen this one yet, and I hear it's really good. It's all taken underwater."

The chimes sounded, the doors swooshed closed, and the SkyTrain moved away, leaving them standing alone on the platform.

"I can't believe this. We left the train. We just got on it. We didn't even go one stop."

"You're going to enjoy it. I know it. This way."

She nearly dragged him out of the station, up the escalator, and toward the convention center. They walked slowly up the stairs and down the long side of the convention center until the arrived at the entrance to the Skyview Theater.

From a distance, Molly squinted to read the board above the ticket booth which showed the features and times. She shook his elbow when she found what she wanted. "Oh! We're in luck. The one I want to see starts in half an hour. We can buy our tickets now and enjoy the scenery for a while. It's really pretty from up here, isn't it?"

"Where are we?"

"This is the Burrard Inlet. We just crossed it on the SeaBus. Over there, see? And that way is Stanley Park."

"I knew that. I meant this place."

The wind ruffled his hair as he turned to look down the inlet. She imagined he could have been a pirate, facing into the wind off the bow of his ship, ready to experience yet another adventure. The only thing that marred the image of a brave adventurer was that one sleeve of his jacket hung empty, and she could see the cast and sling peeking through the opening. Molly wondered what pirates did in days of old when they broke an arm.

"It's called Canada Place. It was built for Expo '86, but now it's Vancouver's biggest convention center. And the Skyview Theater is part of the complex."

He leaned over the railing, three stories above the water, inhaled deeply, and closed his eyes as another ocean breeze ruffled his hair. "There's nothing like this where I come from."

"I think we should go buy the tickets now. We don't want to miss out on getting great seats." She started to reach for her purse, but Ken's hand on her arm stopped her.

"Please, it's my treat. And don't embarrass me by insisting."

Molly snapped her mouth shut. As if she needed more reminders. The difference this time was that here she could put the tickets on her credit card, especially now that she knew exactly how much, or rather how little, she had in her wallet.

Instead of waiting inside for the show to start, they returned to the railing to enjoy the view and the fresh sea breeze. Fighting the chill of the wind, Molly wished she had worn a warmer jacket but wasn't willing to give up the delight of the moment. She struggled to control a shiver but couldn't. After a very poorly suppressed shudder, she crossed her arms and hunched her shoulders.

Ken stepped closer, and she thought he was about to suggest they go inside since he couldn't do up his jacket because of the cast. To her surprise, he slipped his arm around her shoulders and pulled her close. She fit neatly into the opening of his unbuttoned jacket, with the hardness of his cast pushing gently against the side of her waist. She looked up and opened her mouth to protest, but no sound came out as he grinned down at her.

"You looked cold. One thing I've learned so far is that you West Coast people don't know how to dress for cool weather. I'd bet you don't own a pair of boots, either, do you?"

All Molly could do was shake her head. She no longer felt the cold. It was true, the size of him sheltered her from the wind, but the heat generated came from within.

"See? And you're keeping me warm now, too, since I couldn't do my jacket up."

She knew they were supposed to be checking out the scenery, but she continued to look up at him.

His voice lowered in pitch, and he nuzzled his face into her hair. "We're good together, Molly."

Molly's heart hammered in her chest. He was right. They were good together, and not just to keep warm. He kept her disorganized habits in place, and she loosened him up. He quieted her down, and she brought his gentle nature to life. They laughed at the same things, and the same issues upset them both. She liked being with him. She simply liked him. A lot. More than liked. She loved him.

And then he kissed her temple through her hair.

Her heart skipped a beat, then started up in double-time as the force of her thoughts hit her smack between the eyes. She did love him. If she turned her head just a little and lifted her chin, she could allow him to kiss her properly. And if that happened, without moving too much, she could turn and slip her arms under his jacket and hug him and kiss him right back.

The cool wind on the other side of her head ruffled her hair.

Molly stiffened. What was she doing? They were outside a major public attraction, in front of a bunch of people, all strangers.

And Ken was her boss. She couldn't love him.

Molly stepped back. Immediately she missed his warmth. "We should go in now," she stammered.

Once inside, Molly headed straight for the concession.

"Surely you're not going to tell me after all the food you've consumed today, you're hungry."

Her stomach churned. Maybe if she ate some junk food, it would calm her down. She selected the cheapest candy in the display and carefully counted the exact change to the clerk, leaving exactly two cents in her wallet. "No, but you can't watch a movie without a snack. It's just not right. It's a rule."

He didn't say a word, but she could imagine what he was thinking. Candy in hand, Molly directed him toward the entrance to the theater room, where two ushers were distributing the special 3-D glasses to patrons as they entered.

Ken groaned softly. "Oh, no. Don't tell me everyone is going to be wearing those horrible green and red glasses."

He almost stopped walking, but Molly pushed him from behind, determined to focus all her attention to the upcoming movie instead of Ken and what he was doing to her system. "You really haven't been to one of these before, have you? They're not red and green. They look just like regular sunglasses. And the movie is in beautiful bright vivid color. Just as good as a regular movie, only better because you could swear that some of the stuff is almost in your lap. It's a real experience."

Ken mumbled something under his breath Molly couldn't hear, so she ignored him.

The short line inched forward, taking them along with it. They received their 3-D glasses and found their seats.

Ken wiggled the arms of the glasses and held them up to the light. She tried not to laugh at his incredulous expression as he examined them. "These are cardboard. And they're green. Both sides are the same. Are you sure about this? Is this some kind of joke?"

"Trust me. It's different when you're wearing them. Just be patient, okay?"

Before the lights dimmed, Molly struggled to open the bag of licorice, concentrating intently on the little perforated line that was supposed to make it easy. The plastic stretched but refused to tear, making her think that if she couldn't find a pair of scissors in her purse, she should ask for her money back, especially since she'd spent the money she was supposed to have used for her fare home on the candy. She froze for a second as it dawned on her that now she was going to have to borrow more money from Ken to get home. She tugged at it again, on the verge of desperation when Ken spoke.

"I still don't notice anything any different. Everything's just darker."

Molly gave it another pull, only succeeding in stretching it worse. "They're polarized or something. I don't know how they work. All I know is that they do."

She lowered her head, raised the bag, and opened her

mouth, ready to rip it open with her teeth.

"I told myself when I got my laser surgery that I would never wear glasses again, not even sunglasses. Look what you've done to me."

With her mouth wide open and teeth bared mere inches from the bag, Molly paused from her mission and raised her eyes to study him. Ken sat beside her, already wearing the large cardboard 3-D glasses. He scanned the surrounding area, alternately looking through the glasses, then picking them up so the arms remained sitting on his ears, holding the lenses above the level of his eyebrows as he studied the area without looking through them.

"What are you doing?" she whispered between her teeth.

He let the glasses fall back to rest on his nose and turned to her, grinning like a little boy. He scrunched up his nose, making the glasses rise on his cheeks temporarily and drop once more.

Molly's heart skipped a beat. The man was still good-looking wearing oversized cardboard glasses.

They slid down his nose, and he pushed them back into place with his index finger. "So much for my dignified image. Have you ever seen a vice president with cardboard glasses?"

"Vice president?" Molly glanced around the theater, which was rapidly filling up. She wasn't aware Quinlan Enterprises had a vice president. She scanned the crowd around them once more. "There's no one from work here. The only one I know here is. . ." Her voice trailed off. "You. . . ," she whispered.

She stared at him. His 3-D glasses were crooked, and he was still grinning. "What?" he asked.

Suddenly things she'd heard started falling into place. She'd known the production manager's position was safe from being replaced, as was everyone in the office. The only person who would be leaving within a few months was Mr. Rutcliffe, who was about to retire. Everyone knew Ken wasn't going to take that position because Mr. Rutcliffe's assistant was being trained for the job and was doing well, and Ken had nothing to do with either one of them. It all suddenly made sense.

It was Ken. Ken was going to be the vice president. That was the big shake-up rumor said would be happening. Rumor also had it that the senior Mr. Quinlan would be retiring in a few years. And when a president left, it was natural that a vice president stepped up to take his place. Even though he was only twenty-seven years old, Ken was being set up to be the future president of Quinlan Enterprises.

She had fallen in love not only with her immediate supervisor but also with the man who was soon going to run a national corporation. And when that' happened, she, and all the rest of the staff, would be calling Ken "Mr. Quinlan." Molly felt sick.

"Say something. At least tell me how ridiculous I look. But don't sit there with your mouth open."

Molly snapped her mouth shut. All she could do was stare at Ken, who still wore a devastatingly attractive grin beneath the oversize cardboard glasses.

The lights dimmed.

The entire theater stilled and all was quiet. Except her heart. It was pounding so hard surely the erratic thumping echoed through the whole place.

A deep voice boomed through the speaker system; spotlights illuminated the speakers and screens and the cameras in the rear of the large room in sequence as the narrator gave the audience a tour of the workings of the Skyview Theater, saving Molly from having to comment.

"This is fascinating," Ken whispered in her ear. "I can't believe all this technology for a movie."

"Yeah," Molly mumbled over the bag, now firmly clenched in her teeth while she tugged at it increasingly harder. All the electronic wizardry in the world wasn't helping her get the sugar she needed so desperately. At the moment she didn't care if she pulled out a tooth—she needed that candy. She was almost ready to scream when it finally gave way, except she was pulling so hard the wrapper tore completely in two, and red licorice nibs flew into the air and landed on everyone around her.

"Mommy! Mommy! It's raining candy!"

People around her stared, and the mother hushed the child while the demonstration continued.

Molly shrunk down into her chair, hunched as low as she could. She could hear Ken's muffled laughter beside her as he picked a handful out of his lap. He leaned toward her, then deposited a small handful into her open palm. "Here. It's not exactly manna from heaven, but I managed to recover a few."

She mumbled a thank you and prepared herself to watch the show with her diminished supply of candy as the opening credits and film's title expanded in huge, full 3-D across the screen.

"Wow. This really works. Look at the letters. They seem to pop right off the screen. These green glasses are really something."

Since everyone around her started to become engrossed in the effects in front of them, Molly straightened, determined to enjoy the show, except her mind went blank.

As the movie unfolded, many people reached out as if they could actually touch the images they saw. Everyone in the theater flinched when one of the fishes in the presentation jumped out of the water and the 3-D effects made it appear it was going to land in the viewer's lap. The entire audience laughed, right on cue, and the movie continued.

About halfway through the feature, Molly felt the light brush of fingertips on her left shoulder. She turned her head to see Ken's arm drift behind her neck, then settle in around her other shoulder.

She turned her head to respond, although nothing she could put into words would come out.

He leaned his head to whisper in her ear. "We're not in the back row, but it is a movie theater. You didn't expect me not to put my arm around you, did you?"

"Well. . ." Still, no words came. She didn't know what to

think. A million jumbled thoughts rolled through her head, and she couldn't concentrate on the movie, despite the spectacular 3-D effects.

She considered her options. She could handle being friends with him, except her definition of friends was apparently very different than his. Between all the hand-holding and the times he'd draped his arm around her, she'd never had any friend touch her so much. She'd certainly never had any of her friends kiss her.

Somehow, the friendship he had in mind involved "courting her properly," whatever that meant. She tried to imagine what it would be like to date him.

While going shopping to the market and movies and volleyball night at church was her style, she doubted those activities would suit the future president of a large and growing corporation. The closest she'd been to attending a high-class affair, not counting the Chamber of Commerce dinner, was when she'd gone with friends to see *Joseph and the Technicolor Dreamcoat* at an upscale live theater presentation at the Queen Elizabeth Theater. The price of the tickets had been horrendous, and while she'd enjoyed the live acting, she'd felt terribly out of place during intermission. A few ladies were wearing gowns that had likely cost more than her entire wardrobe. Aside from attending theater productions she couldn't afford, she had no idea what the rich and famous did for fun, or if they had fun at all.

If she did start dating Ken, how could she face the people she'd worked with for the past five years? The people who had come to be her friends. The people who would, despite their best intentions, soon begin to hate her for anything they would perceive as favoritism from the boss, especially when plans for Ken's position were announced. She couldn't blame anyone who did, because if the situation were reversed, she would probably feel the same.

There had already been rumors concerning her time spent alone with Ken, so already her reputation was becoming questionable. She couldn't allow her good reputation, or Ken's, to become sullied.

They belonged in separate worlds. Everything about him shouted class and position, education, dignity, and grandeur. Molly liked her casual and laid-back lifestyle; her one-room apartment was great because it was less area to keep clean.

And what if she threw caution to the wind and dated him anyway? What if it didn't work out? How could she work with him? After Robbie's relationship with her boss's son ended in disaster, Robbie had been promptly fired. Would Mr. Quinlan fire her when she and Ken broke up? If he didn't, she couldn't see having to work side by side with Ken every day, especially if he was to be the future president. She'd have to quit before she was fired.

She'd almost worked herself into a sweat when Ken's fingers moved on her shoulder, reminding her that she sat snuggled into his arm. She wondered if his periodic movements were involuntary, or if he was doing it on purpose to remind her that his arm was indeed around her, apparently to stay.

In front of her in panoramic glory, fishes swam, birds flew, and underwater plants swayed. It all went by in a blur. Ken gave her shoulder another gentle squeeze, a tender and very personal touch reminding her once again that he considered this a date. When they left this morning, she had considered their day together to be a friendly outing showing a tourist around town. Was this what he meant by courting her? She'd never been courted before, nor did he have to go through the effort. She was already madly in love with him. Except it wouldn't work. They were all wrong for each other.

"Molly?" Ken's voice whispered in her ear. "Look at me for a second."

He drew his arm away, but instead of sitting back in his chair and letting his arm drop into his lap, his fingers brushed her chin, tipping it up slightly. "The movie is almost over. May I kiss you while it's still dark?"

It was nice of him to ask, except he didn't give her an opportunity to answer. Without removing the cardboard glasses, he tilted his head and kissed her, slowly and gently, and with such a tender sweetness Molly resented the slow brightening of the house lights which caused them to separate.

He backed up slowly, released her chin, and removed his 3-D glasses. His open and unguarded expression made Molly want to kiss him again, but she didn't dare.

His voice seemed deeper than usual, with a delightful low and husky quality she'd never heard before from him. "This movie was a wonderful idea. Thank you for suggesting it."

Molly couldn't move. She became aware that Ken had reached up and was slowly pulling the 3-D glasses off her face. He let them fall into his lap, then brushed her cheek with the backs of his fingers.

Here he was, her Mr. Right. He'd been right under her nose and she hadn't noticed. But how could her Mr. Right be so Mr. Wrong?

The people beside her stood, ready to leave, forcing Molly to pay attention to what was going on around her. They stood and prepared to exit the theater. Ken carried both pairs of glasses and dropped them into the bin as they left. The second they walked outside into the cool night air, his hand grasped hers, and they followed the crowd to the SkyTrain station.

They barely said a word the entire journey home, and Molly didn't force it. She didn't want to spoil the moment. In one short day, everything had changed. Yesterday, they were simply friends. Today they were. . .she didn't know. Either way, whatever it was had to be over before it began. As much as she enjoyed his romantic attentions, she needed his friendship back.

As before, he escorted her up the elevator, through her apartment building, and waited quietly beside her while she unlocked her door. He stepped inside, confirmed there had been no intruders in their absence, and Molly accompanied him back to the door.

Before she met Ken she'd never been lost for words, but again words evaded her. Just how did a woman tell the man she loved that it wasn't going to work, that they could only be friends and nothing more?

She didn't know if it was good or bad that they would still be together all day at work, but at work, it was business. No tender touches and, especially, no kissing. The thought nearly broke her heart, but not nearly as much as not being able to see him again. Perhaps functioning at the office side by side she would see enough of him to enjoy his company, yet abide by the rules of office etiquette to keep a safe distance.

Ken stepped closer, and Molly gulped. She was already backed against the wall in the small entranceway and had nowhere to go, short of sliding against the wall and retreating in fear.

Mere inches separated them. She didn't know what she expected him to say, but he surprised her when he didn't say anything. Without a word or preamble, he kissed her exactly the same way he had kissed her in the theater, only this time, they didn't have to worry about the house lights coming on, or crowds of people around them.

She didn't want the beauty of his kiss to stop. Molly knew this would be the last time she kissed him and the last time she could see him away from the office. It was too dangerous to her heart. Throwing caution aside, she slid her arms under his jacket and kissed him back with all the love in her heart.

When he finally backed up, Molly needed to catch her breath, and it appeared Ken had the same problem.

He still didn't say anything.

Molly hoped by the time they saw each other next at work, they wouldn't be so tongue-tied.

He brushed a light kiss to her cheek. "Good night, Molly. I'll be here at the usual time tomorrow." And he turned and left, shutting the door behind him.

Molly blinked at the closed door. *Tomorrow?* Tomorrow was Sunday.

She hunched her shoulders and buried her face in her hands.

Tomorrow was Sunday, and he was coming to church with her, and there was nothing she could do about it.

sixteen

Molly didn't know how she did it, but she made it through Sunday relatively unscathed. She groaned and sank against the door after Ken left, trying to will her heart to stop pounding.

He'd picked her up right on time, dressed in his casual best for church, proudly announcing the lack of a tie. After church she'd almost forgotten about the youth group's fundraising luncheon, but Ken hadn't. Most of the congregation retreated into the foyer to talk while the teens set up the banquet tables and laid out the food. Everyone else brought a contribution for the potluck lunch except her.

Gwen suggested that word of her cooking skills had leaked out, and that was why she hadn't been asked. Ken joined all her friends in teasing her about it, although in the end he was the only one who defended her culinary talents. He especially enjoyed talking with Garrett. And the whole time, Ken faithfully held onto her hand. She couldn't pull away in front of everyone without worrying about hurting his feelings, so she managed to convince herself to enjoy his company for one more short day.

Except the day wasn't very short.

Somehow, after the banquet, they'd ended up back at Robbie and Garrett's house. Again, Ken got distracted talking to Gwen, the difference this time was that Molly had participated in the conversation, having no choice because he was still holding her hand.

They ordered pizza for supper and attended the evening service, followed by dessert and coffee at a nearby coffee house. They'd had a wonderful day together from practically sunrise to well after sunset.

He was finally gone, but not before he'd kissed her with

153

such intensity that it rocked her to her soul.

She had a wonderful day with him.

She couldn't let it continue.

Molly went to bed but spent most of the night staring up at the ceiling.

≈

Ken smiled as he waited for his computer to boot up. The love of his life was due to walk in the door in seven minutes, and he could hardly wait.

Things were going perfectly. He'd spent another day at her side, most of it with her soft, tender hand enclosed in his. They'd enjoyed their time together, and when the day ended with a heart-stopping kiss, he knew future happiness was within his grasp. In only a few weeks the cast would be off, and he would be able to hold her properly. Life was good.

He knew he was beaming ear to ear when she sat down at her desk, right beside his, but he couldn't help it. It wouldn't be much longer and he would ask for Molly's hand in marriage, and then the world would know they were together.

"Good morning, Molly."

She sat with her head bowed, shuffling a stack of paper. "Oh, good morning," she mumbled, not lifting her head.

Ken turned away and returned to his work. If Molly was still going to be sensitive about the rest of the staff's reaction to them as a couple, he would respect her wishes, although her less than enthusiastic greeting stung.

She didn't speak much to him all morning.

She didn't want to go out for lunch.

She was away from her desk a good part of the afternoon.

She was taking things a little too far.

By the end of the day, Ken was ready to scream. She was ready to leave. Without him.

"Molly? Would you like to go out for dinner?"

"Dinner? Tonight?"

"Do you have other plans?"

She stiffened and glanced from side to side, and her posture relaxed when she saw they were alone in their corner of the office. "No, I don't have other plans. That would probably be a good idea. I think we should talk."

Ken narrowed one eye. Talking was exactly what he had in mind; however, from Molly's reaction, he didn't think they were going to be talking about the same thing.

"Leave your car here. We'll pick it up later."

"Later? But. . ." She shrugged her shoulders. "Okay, I guess so."

The entire drive to the restaurant, he had a sinking feeling in the pit of his stomach. All through the meal, every time the conversation gave indications of drifting to serious topics, he quickly steered the discussion to more pleasant subject matter. As well, every time conversation lagged, he made sure to introduce a new topic, keeping things as animated as he could. He'd never talked so much in his life.

She appeared to be enjoying their evening together, but he didn't want to give her a chance not to. He ended the evening much sooner than he would have preferred in order to quit while he was ahead.

He mentally kicked himself for pushing her to leave her car at the office, because this would give them no opportunity for some privacy to kiss her good night properly. He respected Molly too much to kiss her in middle of the company parking lot.

To his relief, after much protest, he convinced her to allow him to follow her home so he could ensure her safety. When they arrived at her building, after escorting her up the elevator, he quickly checked her apartment for intruders, then left with only a quick peck to her cheek before she had a chance to say anything.

Ken started his car, then smacked the steering wheel with his fist. This was the first and last time he intended to play silly games. Tomorrow, things would be different.

ꝣ

Molly pulled into her parking space and fought back a yawn

as she turned off the engine. After yet another sleepless night, she still couldn't figure out what happened. For all her intentions, she never got a chance to tell Ken that she couldn't see him again outside of work. He'd been funny, witty, charming, and everything she'd ever dreamed of in the perfect male. Except he was her boss and out of her league. He'd been the perfect gentleman, and she'd fallen even more in love with him, if that were possible.

She craned her neck to check her makeup for signs of smears in the rearview mirror, then entered the office building. Around her, conversations hushed as she headed for her desk. She heard a few badly muffled shushes and a short giggle. It gave her a bad feeling, solidifying even more the reasons she shouldn't be in any type of relationship with Ken. She'd worked too hard and too long to let everything come crashing down around her.

The first place she checked on her way to her desk was Ken's area, but fortunately he wasn't there; he was in his uncle's office. She tried not to appear too relieved, because she could feel people watching her as she approached, even though some were pretending to concentrate too intently on their work for first thing in the morning.

Then she saw it. A crystal bud vase containing a single rose sat on her desk. It didn't take a lot of guessing to know who it was from, even though there was no card. Molly plunked herself into her chair and stared at the flower.

Ken's voice drifted from his uncle's office. "Oh, good. You're here. I need you to type up a quick confidential memo for me."

The second she walked into Mr. Quinlan's office, Mr. Quinlan left, shutting the door behind him, leaving her alone with Ken. She didn't have to turn around to know that half the office was straining to see through the open miniblinds to check out what was going on.

She cleared her throat and stiffened her posture. "Before we get started, I want to talk to you about the flower."

"Ah, yes." He smiled, making Molly's foolish heart flutter. "It was a difficult decision between that rose and another blossom I couldn't identify but smelled quite pleasant. I thought the rose suited you better. I hope you like roses."

"Oh, of course I like roses, they're my favorite flower, especially that two-tone kind you picked. I think that variety is called. . . Hold on. Quit distracting me." Molly stepped closer, then, remembering the curious stares of the rest of the staff, backed up again. "You shouldn't have done that."

"Why not? Men send flowers to women at work all the time. There's no rule that says because we work together I can't send you flowers. While on company property we have certain decorum to adhere to, and I have no intention of crossing that line during working hours. As much as I hate to say it, if you received flowers at the office from another man, you'd accept them and enjoy them all day, wouldn't you?"

"Well, of course I would." Not that any man had ever sent her flowers at work, but she assumed she would enjoy them.

"Then don't you think that's logical to do the same when it's from me?"

"Well. . .I guess so."

His self-satisfied smile told Molly she just lost. Except she had a beautiful rose on her desk to enjoy, from the man she'd fallen in love with.

"So enjoy the rose." His grin widened. "And think of me when you look at it."

Molly opened her mouth to protest but gave up. He wanted her to think of him, as if she could ever forget. "Have I just been bamboozled?"

He grinned again and checked his watch at the same time. "That depends on your perspective."

Molly couldn't help herself; she checked her watch at the same time.

"I have a meeting in half an hour. We'd better get that memo done."

He was gone for most of the day, which made Molly wonder

if that were the reason he'd sent the flower, although she had the impression he really hadn't planned on being gone so long. Whenever she thought no one was looking, she reached out to touch the soft, silky petals and inhale the heady fragrance, then pushed the vase back to the corner of her desk.

It was beautiful and so romantic, and it did make her think of him.

And again, she didn't get the chance to tell him they shouldn't see each other, because he'd told her that while at work, they would stick to strictly business.

She didn't want to think about what would happen after work.

She didn't get any choice. Ken finally arrived back at the office at nearly quitting time, obligating her to stay overtime to type his notes from the meeting as he dictated them. He didn't want to take the chance of forgetting anything overnight since he had nothing written down. By the time they finished, they were the last ones remaining in the building except for the janitorial staff.

"I owe you for staying so late. May I buy you dinner?"

"You bought me dinner yesterday."

"Okay, then this time you can buy me dinner."

Molly opened her mouth, but nothing came out.

"Just kidding, Molly. I'm going to put it on my expense account. Let's go."

She studied him as he stood in front of her. After typing his notes, she knew it had been a critical and laborious meeting. Dark circles shadowed his eyes, alluding to a poor night's sleep in addition to a stress-filled day. Yet, he would still take her to a fine restaurant, be a perfect date, and she knew she would enjoy herself thoroughly, even if he almost fell asleep in his plate.

"Maybe this isn't such a good idea. You look so tired. Maybe we should both just go home."

"We both have to eat. And I'm sure not cooking."

The words were out before she had a chance to think about

them. "Then why don't you come over to my place, and I'll cook something simple for the two of us."

He shook his head. "I can't ask you to do that, as much as I appreciate it. You've cooked for me so often I'd feel guilty. But I am tired. Why don't we pick up something fast and take it to Uncle Walter and Aunt Ellen's place? We can put our feet up and relax. They'll be in the den watching television; they won't intrude."

It was the perfect opportunity. She followed him to the house, trying very hard not to compare her visit this time with the only other time she'd been there, which was they day she broke Ken's arm.

She failed. When she walked in the door, being in the exact same setting with the marble tiled entranceway that met rich burgundy carpet, the grand winding staircase, the vast room and fine furnishings, it all came back in a rush. Walter Quinlan, the man who owned the company, at least for now, the man who signed her paychecks, owned this magnificent house, and she was with his favorite relative, his only nephew.

Because of her, Ken had been hurt. Both Mr. and Mrs. Quinlan had fussed over him that day when she brought him home from the hospital. His aunt had nearly burst into tears as Ken bravely tried to conceal his pain, despite the fact that everyone knew how badly he was hurt.

Ken opened the closet, but before he could reach for her coat, she removed her own hanger and hung up her coat by herself. Molly's heart clenched to watch him struggle to hang up his own coat, trying to hold it sufficiently open with the fingers sticking out of the cast at waist height while he worked the hanger into the sleeves. She wanted to take the coat and hanger from his hands and do it for him but knew that since he needed help with so much, he wanted to do whatever he could by himself. The whole procedure appeared so awkward she nearly broke into tears. She couldn't imagine all of what he was going through from day to day, all because of her.

He picked up the bag of food and Molly followed him into the kitchen. His aunt made a brief appearance, then left them alone, which Molly greatly appreciated. After pausing for a prayer of thanks, they began to eat. Despite the obvious luxury of the kitchen, which matched the rest of the house in mood and expert decorating, it felt kind of homey, even comfortable, in an extravagant sort of way.

She didn't want to get comfortable with Ken. She needed to tell him, today, that this could not continue, before she got past the point of no return and disaster struck when he realized how unsuited they were.

"This isn't right. Your first time as my guest, and we're sitting like this in the kitchen. I should have set the dining room table and lit some candles."

Molly turned her head to observe the corner of the elegant dining room through the doorway and tried to imagine eating fast-food hamburgers in such a setting. She could picture a stark white lace tablecloth over the dark wooden table, the lights dimmed, and rather than the standard cliché of sitting across the table lengthwise from each other, they would be sitting side by side.

The candlelight would reflect in Ken's dark blue eyes, making them shimmer as he gazed lovingly into her eyes. He would smile, and she would smile back, just like in an old movie. He would be wearing a tux with a pristine white shirt and she would be wearing a flowing white gown, and then he would tell her that he loved her as much as she loved him. Violin music would sing its haunting strains in the background, and lovebirds would twitter in the air.

The muffled thwack of the fridge door, followed by a soft clunk in front of her broke Molly out of her dreamland.

"Sorry, I forgot you like catsup with your fries. Here you go."

Molly blinked, hard, as she came back to reality with a thud. They were sitting in the kitchen, the catsup bottle sat on the table in front of her.

"Uh, thanks." She opened the lid and squeezed a blob of catsup onto the corner of the plate. She'd never eaten fast-food fries on a plate in her life.

Ken plucked off the top bun of his burger and picked out the pickles, popped them in his mouth, then reassembled his burger.

She could relate to the way he ate a hamburger.

Molly shook her head. She didn't want Ken in her idealistic romantic fantasies, and she didn't want to like the way he ate. She wanted to find something about him that she didn't like, something she could focus on to make ending things easily. She couldn't think of a single thing, except that maybe his nose was a little too big.

Molly swirled a few fries in the blob of catsup. "You shouldn't have given me that flower at work, you know."

"You spend more time at work than at home, so I gave it to you where you would see it the most."

She narrowed one eye. "That's not what I meant. I meant you shouldn't have given it to me in the first place."

"Sure I should have. I wanted to give you a little something special."

Special. She didn't want anything special from Ken, little or big. He was too easy to fall in love with; she didn't need help or encouragement. It had happened without realizing it, and now it was too late. It couldn't continue.

"I don't know what you're trying to do, but this isn't going to work."

"I disagree."

Molly shook her head. "You're so focused. You've got your whole life planned; you have solid goals that you've been working on for years. You're so organized, and I'm. . ." She glanced around the massive pristine home he felt so comfortable in and compared it to her one-room apartment. If no one that she knew of was coming over, her floor was littered with books and magazines, a few stray socks, and other odds and ends. She tried to set the futon back into a couch when she wasn't running late but often forgot to put her pillow away. She usually dusted and vacuumed once a week but frequently forgot. And she did her grocery shopping the day after she ran out of food. ". . .I'm not."

"I know that. It makes you more interesting."

"And look at you!" She waved one hand in the air. A blob of catsup from the fry she was holding splatted onto her plate. Before more dribbled, she shoved it into her mouth. "You're the most comfortable in those custom-tailored suits, perfectly pressed, with perfectly matched ties. My favorite clothes are a five-year-old T-shirt and jeans with a hole in the knee."

Ken smiled halfheartedly. "Opposites attract?"

"And another thing." She waved both hands in the air, now that both were free. "How can I face the people I've worked with for five years? You're going to run the company. Probably own it one day! You know how people talk. I've already heard some wild rumors about our hot relationship."

The halfhearted grin turned to a full smile. "Hot relationship?"

Molly rested her hands on her hips and glared at him.

He patted his tie, cleared his throat, and controlled the smile. "You don't have to worry about what people will say. When we get married, you won't have to work at all, unless you want to. And you wouldn't necessarily have to work here."

"What!?"

"If you felt awkward, I wouldn't mind if you quit and went elsewhere to work. I'd understand."

"Married!?"

He shook his head then rose to his feet. "I'm sorry—I'm doing this all wrong." Very slowly, he turned her swivel chair so she now sat facing him. With his hand resting lightly on the wall for balance he sank to one knee and, once aptly positioned, reached out to grasp her left hand with his right. "I love you, Molly McNeil. Will you marry me?"

All Molly could do was stare at him. He couldn't love her.

It had been easy to fall in love with him, and she imagined that many women before her had fallen for his kind and gentle ways. She couldn't imagine how he could possibly have fallen in love with her.

"This can't be happening. There's a logical explanation for this. Everything in your life is all mixed up, and you're just a little confused. It's a psychological reaction. You know. The shock of breaking your arm, being uprooted and thrown into staying with your aunt and uncle, the move to a completely different city halfway across the country, the new job and enormous responsibilities. Soon you'll settle into a new routine and be able to think more clearly. It's all been too overwhelming for you."

He shook his head and squeezed her hand gently. "No, Molly. I'm thinking very clearly, more clearly than in my entire life. I love you, and I want you to marry me."

Molly yanked her hand away. "No! It isn't right." She jumped to her feet, sending the chair skidding back behind her. "I can't. You don't."

Ken rested his hand on the wall for support and rose to his feet. "I do, Molly."

His choice of words nearly made her heart stop beating. His "I do" echoed through her head. *Wedding words. The ultimate vow of love and devotion.*

"You can't. I've only been going out with you because I felt sorry for you after breaking your arm. We can't see each other any more."

Before she burst into tears in front of him, Molly grabbed her purse off the floor and dashed out of the room and ran through the entrance hallway, slamming the front door behind her.

She ran all the way to the car and took off without taking the time to fasten her seat belt. Before she turned the corner, she glanced in the rearview mirror. The door of the mansion opened, and Ken appeared in the doorway as she drove away.

His shocked expression burned into her heart. But he would see she was right, and he'd get over it.

It was herself that she wasn't sure of.

seventeen

After yet another sleepless night, Molly had never been so bleary-eyed in her life. If this was what is was like to be in love, she wanted no part of it.

Through all the hours of staring up at the ceiling in the dark, she had come to a decision. She was wrong. At first she thought it would be better to work with Ken and keep their relationship to strictly business rather than never see him again. Now she knew different. She couldn't work with him. She couldn't see him every day and ignore the pain of wanting what she couldn't have, or worse, working with him day after day, pretending everything was okay, when her life would never be okay again. As soon as he settled in and made some friends in his own social status, he would find his real true love, and Molly knew she couldn't bear the pain of watching that happen.

She had to leave the job she loved to keep her sanity. Except, since she couldn't afford to be without an income, she would request to be relieved of her duties as Ken's assistant and return to her position as receptionist, which was the farthest away she could be, yet remain in the same building. For as long as she could, she had no alternative but to suffer through each day until she found employment elsewhere.

When she walked into the main office on her way to her desk, Ken's chair was conspicuously vacant. Fortunately, no one watched her as she approached her desk, and all appeared normal. Molly knew different. Life would never be normal again.

She hung up her coat and headed for her desk, then froze momentarily as Mr. Quinlan's office door opened. Ken walked out, but instead of turning toward his desk, he continued walking. He did not approach her, but Molly was close enough to notice the dark circles under his eyes and his bleak expression as he walked into Nancy's vacant office and closed the door.

"Molly, can I see you in my office, please?"

Molly flinched at the sound of Mr. Quinlan's voice. This was the perfect opportunity to make her request, yet she wanted to run and hide.

Molly stiffened her posture and continued walking.

As she lowered herself into the chair, memories roared through her mind of the day she was called into Mr. Quinlan's office and assigned to be Ken's assistant. How suave and sophisticated, yet friendly and gentle he was when they first met. How she'd immediately liked him, how well they worked together. How deeply and honestly he lived his faith and the excellent example he'd been. Most of all, how quickly she'd fallen completely and totally in love with him. The words of his proposal and the picture of how he lowered himself to one knee as he professed his love and proposed marriage flashed through her mind.

Mr. Quinlan sat before her, her personnel file in his hand. "Effective immediately, you will be returning to your position of receptionist. You've done an admirable job, and your efficiency will be noted for future reference. Next time an opening comes up, you will be given first consideration."

Molly's stomach clenched. The possibility of a promotion was now in sight. At one time, it was exactly what she wanted, but now that the moment was upon her, she felt no sense of triumph or accomplishment. Two minutes ago, all she wanted was to get her old job back. Now she had it, and the victory was hollow.

Mr. Quinlan continued. "If you're wondering the reason, Kenneth has requested a transfer back to the Winnipeg office, and he will be leaving tomorrow."

Molly gulped. "Tomorrow?"

Mr. Quinlan nodded. "Yes. He's booking his flight now."

Molly's breath caught. She wouldn't be able to work with him, but she hadn't contemplated that he would be unable to work with her. Typical of Ken, he did nothing in half measures. He was leaving. She would never see him again. Wasn't that what she wanted?

Her mind reeled. He'd worked toward his goal of taking over Quinlan Enterprises since high school. It was his life's ambition. He'd gone to college for this. He'd moved from the place of his birth halfway across the country. He'd left his friends, his family, and his home church. Nothing was more important to Ken than his career.

And he was giving it up. Because of her.

Molly turned her head to stare at the closed door of Nancy's office, knowing Ken was sitting on the other side of it. Ken did nothing on impulse. If he was giving everything up for her, it meant that he really did love her as much as he said he did. It also meant that he had thoroughly thought everything through to its logical conclusions and knew without a doubt that, despite their differences in both personalities and social status, they would be happy. If he said he loved her and wanted to marry her, his decision was not unpremeditated. It wasn't in his nature to do so. He was serious, and she hadn't believed him.

He really did love her, and he had no doubts concerning their future together.

Molly stood so fast she nearly knocked the chair over behind her. "Excuse me, I have to go."

First she had broken his arm, and now she'd broken his heart.

❧

Ken stiffened his back and sucked in a deep breath. He wanted to make his separation from the head office of Quinlan Enterprises as quick and painless as possible. He couldn't believe how his world had come crashing down around his feet in such a short time. Even if Molly didn't love him, he had hoped that one day she possibly could. He would have continued trying to establish a relationship, but when she'd made it abundantly clear her actions toward him were only out of guilt and pity, it had stabbed him where he would never recover.

He couldn't in good conscience terminate her employment, and he certainly couldn't handle being in her presence every day without the pain of defeat and loss of even her friendship. In order to do the admirable and right thing, he had no alternative but to return to his old position and either continue on as production manager at the plant for the rest of his life or seek a management position with another company. He'd chosen to return to what was familiar, at least for now, until he could regain his bearings.

The phone book sat open in front of him to the airline section and Ken began dialing the phone. He flinched as the door burst open, then flinched again when Molly slammed the door shut behind her with a bang.

Molly marched to the front of the desk and thumped the phone book shut. He started to open his mouth, but before he could protest, she grabbed the phone out of his hand and whacked the button down with her finger, knowing full well that due to his lack of mobility because of the cast, he couldn't stop her.

She stood before him, breathing heavily, the phone in her hand.

"Can I help you with something, Molly?"

"I can't allow you to do this. You can't abandon your career." She dropped the receiver into the phone cradle and crossed her arms. Her chest rose and fell quickly with her angered breathing; her mane of unruly hair surrounded her face in a halo of color, the red a testimony to a rising temper.

"I've simply had a change of plans."

He didn't know what he expected Molly to do, but as usual, he wasn't even close. Before he realized what she was doing, she stomped around the desk and stood beside his chair, staring down at him, her clenched fists planted on her hips. She was vibrant and beautiful and he loved her from the depths of his soul and always would.

"I can't let you pack up and leave, you know."

Ken didn't say a word, afraid to guess where the conversation was going, almost afraid to hope for what he knew he couldn't have.

"Your family is counting on you. You've worked up to this your whole life. I know you won't fire me. And you can't make me quit before I'm ready to leave."

"I didn't ask you to do anything."

"You know I can't continue working here if we're going to have any kind of relationship, don't you?"

He knew he should quit while he might be ahead and remained quiet, but his mind reeled and his heart pounded in his chest with the hope she meant what he thought she meant. And if she did mean it, he didn't want to wait.

Ken opened his mouth to speak, but Molly raised one finger in the air, silencing him. He turned his chair to face her and slipped his free hand to her waist as she remained standing before him, almost afraid to touch her, at the same time afraid not to.

Ken stood, inwardly loathing the cast that held his left arm immobile. If there ever was a moment he needed to hold Molly properly, it was now. Since he couldn't wrap his arms around her, he rested his fingers to the side of her waist and cupped her chin with his other hand. He swallowed hard, forcing the words out. "Does this mean you've changed your mind? Will you marry me, Molly? And I don't want a long engagement."

Molly raised her hands, and Ken closed his eyes for a brief second at the gentle touch of her fingers on his cheeks. She raised herself on her toes and brought herself closer. His heart soared as he thought she was going to kiss him. He knew a major portion of the office staff could see them through the office window, but he didn't care. If Molly was touching him in plain view of anyone in the area, it could only mean one thing, that his prayers for the love of the perfect woman were coming true.

"Me neither," she whispered against his lips. Ken closed his eyes, waiting, but Molly spoke again just before she kissed him. "So I guess that means I quit."

A Letter To Our Readers

Dear Reader:

In order that we might better contribute to your reading enjoyment, we would appreciate your taking a few minutes to respond to the following questions. We welcome your comments and read each form and letter we receive. When completed, please return to the following:

Rebecca Germany, Fiction Editor
Heartsong Presents
PO Box 719
Uhrichsville, Ohio 44683

1. Did you enjoy reading *At Arm's Length?*
   ❑ Very much. I would like to see more books
      by this author!
   ❑ Moderately
      I would have enjoyed it more if _____

      _____

      _____

2. Are you a member of **Heartsong Presents**? Yes ❑ No ❑
   If no, where did you purchase this book? _____

   _____

3. How would you rate, on a scale from 1 (poor) to 5 (superior),
   the cover design? _____

4. On a scale from 1 (poor) to 10 (superior), please rate the
   following elements.

   _____ Heroine   _____ Plot

   _____ Hero   _____ Inspirational theme

   _____ Setting   _____ Secondary characters

5. These characters were special because_____

_____

_____

6. How has this book inspired your life?_____

_____

_____

7. What settings would you like to see covered in future **Heartsong Presents** books?_____

_____

_____

8. What are some inspirational themes you would like to see treated in future books?_____

_____

_____

9. Would you be interested in reading other **Heartsong Presents** titles?   Yes ❑   No ❑

10. Please check your age range:
   ❑ Under 18   ❑ 18-24   ❑ 25-34
   ❑ 35-45   ❑ 46-55   ❑ Over 55

11. How many hours per week do you read?_____

Name _____

Occupation _____

Address _____

City _____ State _____ Zip _____

new year, new love

Introducing four brand-new novellas in modern settings that reflect on the anticipation of entering a new year—new calendar, new goals to accomplish, and a new chance at love. Rejoice in the transformation of a young woman in *Remaking Meridith* by Carol Cox. Throughout *Beginnings*, Peggy Darty will have you laughing and crying as two lonely adults are laid up in the hospital over the holiday season. Then, discover how setting goals brings together a church singles' class and sparks the flame of love in *Never Say Never* by Yvonne Lehman. Finally, in *Letters to Timothy*, see how author Pamela Kaye Tracy unites five needy people with one pen pal letter.

paperback, 352 pages, 5 ³⁄₁₆" x 8"

❤ ❤ ❤ ❤ ❤ ❤ ❤ ❤ ❤ ❤ ❤ ❤ ❤ ❤ ❤

❤ ❤ ❤ ❤ ❤ ❤ ❤ ❤ ❤ ❤ ❤ ❤ ❤ ❤ ❤

·····Hearts♥ng·····

Any 12
Heartsong
Presents titles
for only
$26.95 *

CONTEMPORARY ROMANCE IS CHEAPER BY THE DOZEN!

Buy any assortment of twelve *Heartsong Presents* titles and save 25% off of the already discounted price of $2.95 each!

*plus $1.00 shipping and handling per order and sales tax where applicable.

HEARTSONG PRESENTS *TITLES AVAILABLE NOW:*

(If ordering from this page, please remember to include it with the order form.)

········Presents········

Great Inspirational Romance at a Great Price!

Heartsong Presents books are inspirational romances in contemporary and historical settings, designed to give you an enjoyable, spirit-lifting reading experience. You can choose wonderfully written titles from some of today's best authors like Veda Boyd Jones, Yvonne Lehman, Tracie Peterson, Debra White Smith, and many others.

When ordering quantities less than twelve, above titles are $2.95 each.
Not all titles may be available at time of order.

Hearts♥ng Presents
Love Stories Are Rated G!

That's for godly, gratifying, and of course, great! If you love a thrilling love story, but don't appreciate the sordidness of some popular paperback romances, **Heartsong Presents** is for you. In fact, **Heartsong Presents** is the *only inspirational romance book club*, the only one featuring love stories where Christian faith is the primary ingredient in a marriage relationship.

Sign up today to receive your first set of four, never before published Christian romances. Send no money now; you will receive a bill with the first shipment. You may cancel at any time without obligation, and if you aren't completely satisfied with any selection, you may return the books for an immediate refund!

Imagine. . .four new romances every four weeks—two historical, two contemporary—with men and women like you who long to meet the one God has chosen as the love of their lives. . .all for the low price of $9.97 postpaid.

To join, simply complete the coupon below and mail to the address provided. **Heartsong Presents** romances are rated G for another reason: They'll arrive *Godspeed!*